2 E DOCTOR DECIDES

In[...] y caught up in a Mod and Rocker rio[...] argate, lovely ballerina Heather De[...] seriously injured. A wealthy young nig[...]ub proprietor, Ronnie Steele, comes to her ssistance and during her period in hospita his concern and sympathy helps Heathe back to health. The couple fall deep[...] love, but there is a secret in Hea[...] past. Learning that she will no long r e able to dance, she takes empl[...] t in a club, but jealousy leads to hatre[...] la attempted murder. The past shad[...] ather's life again, but the love of the [...] n finds its reward in the end.

THE DOCTOR DECIDES

The Doctor Decides

by

Margaret A. Cole

Dales Large Print Books
Long Preston, North Yorkshire,
BD23 4ND, England.

British Library Cataloguing in Publication Data.

Cole, Margaret A.
  The doctor decides.

  A catalogue record of this book is
  available from the British Library

  ISBN   1-84262-476-8 pbk
  ISBN   978-1-84262-476-0 pbk

First published in Great Britain in 1966 by Robert Hale Ltd.

Published in Large Print 2006 by arrangement with
Robert Hale Limited

Dales Large Print is an imprint of Library Magna Books Ltd.

Printed and bound in Great Britain by
T.J. (International) Ltd., Cornwall, PL28 8RW

To my friends the Dutch editor Hans Roest, his charming wife Joep and their son Désiré, with the author's best wishes for their new life in England!

CHAPTER ONE

As owner of an expensive night club and chairman of eight flourishing companies, Ronald Steele, aged twenty-two, could have afforded a world tour or any expensive and exotic holiday. However, the two years that he had spent in Canada on his uncle's ranch had given him simple tastes. And so he decided to go to Margate for his Whitsuntide holiday. He drove the Humber himself to the coast. He put up at a small but comfortable hotel, The Denham.

As Ronnie sipped his early-morning tea, he recalled a conversation he had had on the previous day with a member of his night club. It had been with Ali Chanderi, a young Indian who performed a conjuring act in the cabaret of The Delkushla, as Ronnie's night club had been named.

Ali had been at the same public school as Ronnie and the two young men had kept up a correspondence during the years that Ronald Steele had spent in Canada.

In response to Chanderi's expostulation,

'But whatever do you want to go to Margate for?' Steele had answered, 'I'm going to Margate because I like watching ordinary folk enjoying themselves on a holiday. Also, I fancy the air of the east coast.'

'Are you going by yourself?'

'Yes.'

Ali had been silent for a moment and had then said, 'I know at least half a dozen Delkushla honeys who would give their eyes to accompany you. A rich, handsome young bachelor, especially one like yourself, who employs such fabulous lovelies, well, you can take your pick. To start with, there are a number of your "Fab Girls" who have a "crush" on their boss.'

Ronnie had laughed and had closed the conversation by saying, 'Ali, *you* ought to know by now I never "mix business with pleasure". As for the night club and the other businesses that my father has left me, well, I wish the dear old boy had lived, because he thoroughly enjoyed being a tycoon and I don't!'

Ali had replied, 'Your father was only fifty when he died, wasn't he?'

'That's right! He was killed in a car crash. I was in Canada at the time. As I think I told you, two years previous to that when I left public school where you and I were educated, I asked Dad "Could I go to my uncle who had a farm in Canada?" At first Dad raised merry hell. You see, he had planned that I should go, first, to a university, and then into one of his businesses. For days he sent me to Coventry because I refused to fall in with his plans! At the end of a week he said:

"'Okay! Go to Canada and see how you like it! After the comfort and luxury you've had all your life you'll soon get sick of the ranch. You're a minor still, my lad, so legally I expect I could insist on your staying in England. However, I'll do this – I'll consent to your going and I'll pay your passage to Canada if you solemnly promise to return to England in three years' time.'"

As Ronnie got out of bed and started dressing he reflected that he *had* kept faith with his parent, because not only had he returned, but he had tried to give his best to his father's enterprises.

Later on, when he went downstairs and handed his bedroom-key in at the reception desk he chatted to the pleasant man at the other side of the counter. The reception-clerk said to Ronnie:

'I hope you don't mind my suggesting this,

11

sir, but if I were you I'd get out of Margate this morning.'

'Get out! But why?'

'Well, I've heard that early this morning about a thousand hooligan-teenagers have arrived in Margate and are already playing merry hell in the town. These fellows consist of two rival gangs. They call themselves Mods and Rockers. A great number arrived in Margate late last night.'

'But I wonder they managed to get accommodation.'

'They *didn't*, sir. I mean, I've heard that a vast number of fellows and girls just slept on the sands all night. When our milkman delivered his milk here this morning he told some of the hotel staff that trouble began shortly after dawn. Kiosks were broken into for food and drink. Shops and windows were smashed and beach-huts forced open. Then a gang of about fifty Mods attacked the Rockers on the beach. So if I were you, sir, I'd drive *out* of Margate this morning.'

As Ronnie made his way to the dining-room he glanced at the clock and saw that it still wanted a quarter to nine.

As it was a lovely morning Ronnie longed to get into the sunshine. Consequently he hurried over his breakfast.

12

Mindful of the warning that he had received from the booking-clerk he got his car out of the garage intending to leave Margate.

However, when he drove along by the promenade, curiosity got the better of him. He parked the car by the kerbside. Then, noticing that a number of men and women had risen from their chairs and were now leaning over the promenade rail and were looking down at the beach, he followed their example.

He took a vacant place and then saw that a police sergeant and two constables were standing next to him.

Suddenly a long-haired, dandily dressed youth chased a leather-coated fellow up the steps which led from the beach. A fight started between the two teenagers.

The policemen intervened and forced them apart. One constable said, 'Hi! Break it up, can't ye! Get on your ways! Haven't you fellows any homes to go to?'

Eventually the Mod and the Rocker disappeared from the promenade.

Ronnie had swung around to watch the fight between the Mod and the Rocker. Now he leant over the rail again. He noticed that when the constables were making a move to go down the steps to the beach the sergeant prevented them doing so, saying:

'Stop on the promenade for the present. While we've got them down there they are under our eyes.'

Ronnie looked to his left where two soberly dressed elderly men had been watching the scene on the beach below them. Now one man turned to the other and jerked his head towards two empty deck-chairs which they had probably lately vacated. As he beckoned he said, 'Let's keep out of this, mate! It's nothing to do with us.'

They ambled over to the chairs and sitting down were soon absorbed in their morning papers.

Their going had left a space and across it Ronnie encountered the eyes of a young girl – large, lovely expressive eyes, set in an attractive oval-shaped face. Her forehead was high and beautifully shaped. He noticed her forehead because her dark hair was swept back in front but at the sides hung loosely making a frame for her exquisite face. She was of medium height and on the slight side. He noted the extreme grace of her movements and her well-shaped hands. Ronnie speculated as to her profession. He said to himself, 'Although she wears her clothes beautifully I'm sure she's not a mannequin.'

Ronnie, in his capacity as the owner of an expensive London night club had met a number of beautiful women, but none of them had attracted him like this young girl. 'There's something different about her,' he criticised.

All at once Ronnie remembered the two young hooligans who had attacked each other on the promenade and he instantly became worried in case this beautiful brunette got mixed up in any unpleasantness. He felt that he *must* warn her. Moving near the girl he addressed her, saying:

'Don't you think you'd better go back to your hotel? These young hooligans may cause trouble.'

She gave a start when he spoke to her. He repeated his advice and she answered, 'I'm quite all right, thank you.'

Her tone, though courteous, was very decisive. All at once Ronnie wondered was she waiting for a jealous husband, perhaps the type who would make a scene if he found his wife hobnobbing with a male stranger? He couldn't see the girl's left hand so he didn't know whether she was married or not.

A man dressed like a railway porter suddenly occupied the space between Ronnie and the girl.

The newcomer looked down at the beach and then turned to Ronald Steele, exclaiming, 'These young hooligans and degenerates. They've already had a "go" at wrecking the railway station. They smashed windows and entering the buffet knocked over tables and broke the crockery. However, in the buffet they met their match in the cleaner. She is fifty but is as game as you make 'em. She chased the young swine out – with a *mop!*'

He laughed, and then instantly looked grave and angry again.

'The young thugs,' he continued, 'you ought to just see how they've messed up the place. They and their "birds" have used the sands and the railway carriages as bedchambers, fair disgustin' I call it. I think–'

A noise from the beach interrupted the speaker and attracted the gaze of Ronnie, the dark-haired girl and the others who were leaning over the rail of the promenade.

It was a strange and terrifying sight that met their eyes – fighting had broken out near the toddler-fringed waves – fighting between small groups of Mods and even smaller groups of Rockers. The children on the beach screamed. Mothers snatched their babies and hugged them to their bosoms for protection. Frightened families joined wagon-trains encircled with deck chairs.

Then there was a lull in the fighting. The Rockers got away from the Mods on the lower beach and formed themselves in a group by the wall.

All at once the Mods seemed to be re-assembling. A group of Mods grew to twenty, then thirty, then two hundred.

Without direction, huddling by instinct, they strung themselves out in a four-deep arc like a school photograph, but swaying a little, clapping a little, jeering a little, not at anybody but just jeering. They faced the prom and the deck-chairs where men in pullovers were reading their papers or smoking or just sitting, with their eyes shut, in the sunshine.

Ronnie noticed that the policemen were advancing towards the top of the steps. He heard one of the constables comment on the Mods who were swaying and chanting down below:

'For all the world like a lot of perishing lemmings, the young swine!'

Ronnie longed to get the brunette away

17

from the promenade but he hesitated remembering that she had already rejected his advances and offer of help.

The swaying pack on the sands beckoned and more Mods seemed to appear from nowhere and attach themselves to the braying mob.

They seemed to be drawn by a purpose, though none became apparent. They converged picking their way through the miniature cricket games, the prams and the sleeping grandmas in deck-chairs.

They moved like converts at a Billy Graham rally or as one man on the promenade said like 'drunken dervishes'.

The Mods grew to about three hundred and looked as menacing as any crowd of that size whose purpose is unpredictable.

The watching policemen on the hot promenade waited.

Ronnie leant behind the porter and tapped the girl's arm. She turned around in a startled way.

'Please let me see you back to your hotel.'

'No – thanks!'

She turned her gaze back on the beach. Ronnie felt that for the moment there was nothing he could do. So he resumed his study of the scene on the beach below them.

There had been a stillness.

Suddenly about a dozen youths and their 'birds' broke from the mob of Mods and darted along the beach, the pack of Mods followed, boys and girls running hand in hand, Chelsea boots with Acton heels drumming along the sands.

After a short run of about a hundred yards the leaders turned and the stampede behind paused and reacted. Then it was a race to get back to the original spot where they packed close and went back to their swaying. It was as pointless and as unreal as that.

Meantime the Rockers stood at the far end, in the vicinity of the steps. The leather-jacketed fellows watched and waited.

All at once a whistle shrilled out and the Mods advanced like lightning and made for the Rockers who fled up the steps followed by the pack of Mods.

The whole yelling fighting mob were up the steps and were on Ronnie and the people standing near him.

The sergeant and constables advanced on the screaming hooligans. Some more uniformed men appeared but the police were not only frightfully outnumbered but both Mods and Rockers turned on the policemen and attacked them. The teenagers broke deck-chairs and used pieces of them and also bottles as effective weapons.

Ronnie yelled at the girl, 'Let's get off the promenade. I have my car nearby and will run you to your hotel.'

She made to join him but just at this minute a fleeing Mod charged into the brunette and knocked her on the pavement. The male teenager fled without giving a backward glance at the girl who lay on the pavement.

Ronald pushed his way to the fallen girl at about the same time as a young constable who had witnessed the accident. Both men knelt on the pavement beside the girl.

'She's conscious,' said the officer.

'Yes,' replied Ronnie, 'but she's in pain.'

'It's my right arm. It's hurting terribly.'

Gently Ronnie put his arm around her to support the injured limb. 'I'm afraid to move anyone with an injured arm' – he spoke to the police officer.

'Quite right, sir. The trouble is, the first-aid post is a little way off.'

'If you'll tell me where the hospital is, I have my car near the kerb and I can run her along there.'

'I'll help you with your young lady.'

The constable managed to clear a passage while Ronnie carried the girl to his car. The police officer gave Ronald very clear directions as to the route to the hospital and then the constable hurried off to join his fellow police officers in their fight with the Mods and Rockers.

As they drove along Ronnie tried to comfort his companion.

'Don't be frightened,' he consoled. 'Probably your arm isn't broken. It may only be a strained ligament. Of course, you must be feeling "all out" because you've had a terrible shock and are probably badly bruised. In a few minutes you'll be safe and sound and resting in a hospital bed.'

She tried to thank him, but he prevented her, saying, 'Don't you worry! I'll see to everything. I mean, I can run along to your hotel and fetch back to the hospital anything that you may require like a nightdress, washing things, etc. By the way, is there anyone at your hotel I can bring along to the hospital to you? I mean, did you come down with a companion?'

'No, I came down alone.'

He glanced at her left hand and saw that it was ringless.

After a moment's thought Ronnie said, 'I'm called Ronald, Ronnie Steele. I think it would look better if I gave the hospital authorities your name and the name of your hotel.'

'It's Clovelly and it is not a hotel but a guest house, and I am Heather Dean.'

'Thanks, we ought to be just near the hospital now, so don't worry, Miss Dean, I'll see to everything.'

The Casualty Sister and the doctor who took charge of Heather were pleasant people. They reassured Ronnie.

'Don't worry about your friend, we'll see to her at once. She'll soon be comfortably settled in bed, so you need not wait.'

'I told Miss Dean I would drive to her guest house for her nightwear and anything else she may need.'

'That's very good of you.'

'May I come back and see Miss Dean?'

The nurse smiled. 'Of course! Come at the visiting hours every day. They are from three to four. There is also an evening period.'

Ronald thanked the pleasant nurse and, after finding out what articles Heather would require from her guest house, he set off for Clovelly where he interviewed the proprietress who packed a small bag containing Heather's nightwear, brush and comb and toilet requisites. The owner of Clovelly sent her sympathy and good wishes to the injured girl.

Ronnie left Heather's overnight bag with the porter.

As he drove away from the hospital for the second time, his thoughts reverted to Heather. Although he was used to beautiful women he knew that no one had attracted him so greatly as Heather Dean had attracted him. He was used to women making the running with him on account of his position and his wealth. This young girl had made no attempt to gain his attention, quite the contrary. Although she was so beautiful, she seemed to be unaware of her own attractions. She had a quality of elusiveness which attracted him. Heather also possessed great grace of movement. All this again made him speculate as to the girl's profession. For a number of reasons he made up his mind to postpone his return to London. In that way he could visit Heather every day and so get to know her better.

Back at his hotel he had a quick lunch.

The booking-clerk seemed surprised that Ronnie had returned for lunch. He said:

'So you didn't leave Margate after all?'

'No. I've been busy taking to hospital a victim of the Mods and Rockers.'

The official was deeply interested when

Ronald told him of the events of the morning. In answer to Ronnie's question, 'Do you know the latest about the Mods and Rockers?' he answered:

'Oh yes, sir! I can tell you what has happened in Margate in the last hour or so. Several of the guests and also the members of the hotel staff have brought me in the latest news. I heard that when these hooligans were chased off the promenade they made for the town where they congregated around the Town Hall. There the police surrounded them, and made a number of arrests. The Mods and Rockers who got away from the Town Hall – it is said there were about a hundred of the fellows – rushed around the town breaking and destroying. They made for the Fun Fair and as one of the guests said, "They turned 'Dreamland' into a nightmare". The visitor here, who had been a witness to all this, said that the police slammed the gates and imprisoned about a hundred Mods in the car park. However, a little later another large contingent of Mods came up, stormed the gates, got in and released their fellow Mods. The police made further arrests and the Mods who got away made for the beach again.'

'I noticed that there seemed to be a num-

24

ber of young girls mixed up in this affair.'

'Oh, yes! I've heard that several teenage girls have been arrested.'

'Well, I've had enough of the promenade and streets for one day, so as the hotel has a nice large garden I think I'll get a deck-chair and have a loll in the sunshine.'

'A very good idea, Mr. Steele, and you are not the only one who has got away from the front. I have heard that a number of people have left the beach and the promenade. All this upset seems so hard on people who have only the Whitsun week-end to enjoy the sea and the sunshine.'

'Yes and it's very hard on the day-trippers.'

'I think it's cruel that kiddies should have been driven from the sand and sea by these young swine.'

When Ronnie settled in a deck-chair he started speculating again about the girl who interested him so greatly.

He placed her age about the end of her teens. Again he wondered what Heather's profession could be. She did not suggest either a mannequin, a teacher, an actress, a secretary or a business girl.

It was beautifully warm in the sunshine. Ronnie fell asleep.

Later on he was awakened by the sound of

a waiter's voice saying:

'Would you like your tea brought out into the garden?'

'That *would* be nice. Thank you.'

'Very good, sir!'

Later on Ronnie phoned the hospital and was told that Miss Dean was resting comfortably. In answer to his question the nurse said, 'Yes, Miss Dean has had an X-ray for her right arm.'

Ronnie dined at his hotel. Then as the night was a perfect one he went out and sat on the promenade thinking and smoking.

His chair overlooked the sands. He noticed that a number of boys and girls were lying on the beach, and he thought that these teenagers were probably Mods and their birds or Rockers and their girls. However, everything was still and peaceful.

When he left the front to go into a bar to get a drink the landlord told him that a large contingent of police had arrived in Margate from other towns and that the magistrate who was interviewing the arrested teenagers said that he would give up his Whitsuntide holiday so that the trials of the Mods and Rockers could go on. This chairman of the magistrates was said to have declared, 'I'll give these fellows the maximum sentence.'

'Has there been any more trouble in the last few hours?'

'There have been isolated fights and there is blood on the sands. Just outside this pub, sir, the barman saw two female-Mods fighting and trying to pull out each other's hair. A number of Mods' "birds", as they call themselves, were egging on the fighters. I think, sir, that you came along the front? How is it now on the beach and the promenade?'

'It was all quiet when I left.'

'Well, I hope it keeps like that.'

Ronnie finished up his drink. Then, as it was a lovely night, he was glad to get into the air again.

Later on when he leant over the rail of the promenade a strange sight met his eyes. A group of youths had made a pile of the deck-chairs on the sands and had set a light to them. Then these teenagers danced around the flames chanting as they did so. A number of police constables arrived, surrounded the teenagers and forced the fellows to put out the flames by throwing sand on to the burning pile. Then the police arrested the ring-leaders.

Ronnie went for a short stroll and then made for his hotel.

Before getting off to sleep his last thoughts were of the beautiful girl who had come into his life so unexpectedly and in such a strange way.

CHAPTER TWO

Next day, at breakfast-time Ronald Steele read in his paper an account of the battle between the Mods and Rockers at Margate and of the damage done to the town by these teenagers.

When he had finished his meal Ronnie wondered how he would occupy himself during the morning. After lunch he was going to the hospital to visit Heather Dean.

As he got up from the table the idea occurred to him that it would be interesting to go to the court to see how the presiding magistrate dealt with the Mods and Rockers who had been arrested yesterday.

Accordingly he consulted the friendly booking-clerk as to the route.

The man told him the way and advised, 'If I were you, sir, I'd go early if you want to get into the hall because the court is not large.'

Ronnie left the hotel immediately and got to the magistrates' court in time to be admitted. He heard, later, that instructions had been given to the policeman at the door to restrict the number of entrants, and to debar anyone likely to create a disturbance.

As soon as the chairman of the magistrates entered he warned the people present that anyone who interrupted would be instantly ejected and dealt with severely. He then ordered that all the doors of the court should be locked.

Then followed the business of dealing with the arrested teenagers. There was no disturbance at all. Outside a party of screaming teenagers who tried to approach the building were turned back by *one* policeman.

Ronald Steele was deeply interested in the proceedings. One by one the self-styled Mods and Rockers stood up to be sentenced. And one by one the Whitsuntide Terrors were cut down in size by the grey-haired doctor, the chairman of the magistrates.

Ronnie stayed as long as he could because he was held by the skilful handling of the cases. He heard, later, that fifty-one youths eventually appeared, one by one, in the dock that day.

The police sergeant spoke of the Mods and Rockers campaign which had terrorised the town on the previous day.

The charges were proceeded with and consisted of 'threatening behaviour, carrying offensive weapons, causing injury and assaulting the police.'

A superintendent now took up the tale. 'Two large groups were on the sands. A whistle sounded and the Rockers were chased up the steps leading to the promenade by the Mods. Ten constables with staves drawn contained the Mods, but several of the constables were injured. Later a group went into the High Street and a number of windows were broken and damage inflicted on property and persons in the town.'

The Superintendent added, 'These youths are heroes in a group or to their girl friends but they present a different picture this morning.'

Ronnie studying the accused, saw the truth of the police official's words – the cocky braggarts and bullies of yesterday had turned into untidy and dishevelled shifty and anxious-looking specimens.

Then the chairman of the magistrates, aged sixty-four and father of two grown-up sons, started to deal with the first of the cases. He said:

'It is not likely that the air of this town has been ever before polluted by hosts of hooligans, male and female, such as you are, and we shall see to it that it doesn't happen again.'

The superintendent then elaborated on yesterday's happenings and gave high praise to the constables involved in the case, saying, 'With more than a thousand of these young hooligans moving among the trippers and holiday-makers the police had a major task. The police behaved like heroes and several officers were hurt.'

The magistrate then proceeded to impose sentences. He referred to the accused, whom he designated as:

'These long-haired, mentally unstable, petty little hoodlums, sawdust Ceasars who behave like "rats" and can only find courage when, like rats, they hunt in packs. In so far as this court has been given power we shall discourage thugs of your kind who are infected with the vicious virus.'

He proceeded to sentence. Fines totalling £1,930 were imposed. Five youths were fined £75 each.

Later on, when Ronnie had returned to the hotel, he learnt from one of the staff that while the court had been sitting that morning there had been another outburst of violence between Mods and Rockers and three youths had been stabbed and had been taken to hospital.

After Ronnie had finished his lunch he set off to visit Heather. On the way he stopped at several shops – at a confectioners where he chose a large box of chocolates, at a greengrocers where he bought a bunch of black grapes and lastly at a florists where he purchased some lovely flowers.

Laden with gifts, he drove on to the Margate hospital.

CHAPTER THREE

On the previous evening Ronnie had phoned the hospital and he had been told that Miss Heather Dean was in the Harvey Ward.

A pleasant-looking nurse at the entrance to the ward, in answer to Ronnie's enquiries, pointed out the bed at the far end of the room where the girl he sought was lying.

He noticed that her right forearm was in a plaster-cast. Her face lit up when she saw him.

She was in a sitting position, being propped up by pillows.

'How good of you to come!' she said.

He noticed that, although her voice was a pleasant and musical one, it was not a professionally produced voice, and so he felt that she was not an actress.

When he placed his gifts on the bedside-table she flushed with pleasure and taking the bunch of flowers in her left hand pressed them affectionately to her face, saying, 'What a glorious scent! How can I thank you for these charming gifts?'

Her hands wandered lovingly over the flowers. Again, he was struck by her grace of movement. Her hands seemed to talk. They reminded him of the beautiful fluttering hands of an Indian female performer in a 'Lotus Dance' he had witnessed. Once again he speculated about Heather's profession.

He laughed and replied, 'Please don't thank me for these few things.'

He took the chair she had indicated, and then asked:

'How are you feeling now?'

'Very lazy.' She smiled up at him.

'But how's the arm?'

'Since it was put in a plaster-cast I've had no pain.'

'Is your leg in plaster of paris?'

'No, it's only bruised and cut.'

'Thank goodness for that! Do you sleep well?'

'Yes, but a nurse gave me a sleeping draught, perhaps she thought I wouldn't get off without.'

'Poor girl! You must have had a terrible shock yesterday, to say nothing of the injury to the arm and the pain of the bad bruises.'

She was silent so he went on:

35

'Have you had an X-ray for your arm?'

'Yes.'

'Do you know the results of the X-ray yet?'

'No, but as I've had a plaster-cast put on it, I guess it is a break or a bad fracture.'

She lowered her voice and then continued:

'The girl in the next bed is very friendly. She says that they don't tell the patients much.'

'No, but the hospital authorities will sometimes give confidential information to a relative. Talking about relatives, look!' He took a little packet out of one of his pockets as he spoke. 'Here is a small pad of paper, envelopes and stamps, in case you might want to write a letter.'

'How very thoughtful of you!' She put the packet in her bedside cupboard, remarking, 'The notepaper will be most useful.'

'Well, I thought you might want to write to your father and mother.'

A sad look came on the girl's face. She answered, 'My father and mother are both dead. My only relative is a married uncle who lives in Scotland.'

'And who looks after you?'

She shrugged her shoulders and opened her hands as she replied:

'Myself, I suppose.'

Again he was struck by the grace of her movements. The fact that her hands were ringless pleased him.

He voiced his thoughts. 'You're neither married, nor engaged, I take it?'

'Nor have I got a "steady".'

She laughed again, but he thought that her laughter sounded strained.

He persisted. 'But you *will* want to write some letters?'

'Oh, yes! I want to send a note to Mrs. Spence. She owns the house in which I have a flat. The doctor who put my arm in plaster told me that as my hand isn't injured I can use it as much as possible. As my holiday ends today I must get in touch with Madame Eglantine and tell her about the accident.'

'Should I know who Madame Eglantine is?'

'Madame Eglantine has a well-known school of ballet and I teach dancing there.'

'Have you been there long?'

'Only six months, since I came back from the continental tour with the *corps de ballet*.'

Ronnie's interest in Heather increased.

He said, 'I was trying to puzzle out what was your profession. I ought to have guessed that you were a ballerina.'

Again a sad expression came into the girl's beautiful eyes.

'I have only been in one *corps de ballet* and that was for only a couple of months. I was not re-engaged when the tour started again.'

Ronnie's interest in Heather had grown so considerably that he wanted to say *'Why weren't you re-engaged?'* But he remembered the hurt look in her eyes, so he remained silent.

Heather continued, 'When my contract was not renewed, as I was out of work, I accepted Madame Eglantine's offer to teach dancing at her school.'

Her companion nodded in a sympathetic way. He said, 'Yes, I agree that you *must* let Madame Eglantine know about your accident. To start with there can be no question of your being at her school tomorrow. I can take a safe bet they'll keep you in this hospital for perhaps a week or even weeks. Can Madame Eglantine manage without you?'

'She *will* miss me. You see, Madame has put on a lot of weight and so she leaves the practical part of the work to me.'

'I wonder what she'll do in your absence?'

'She may be able to secure a temporary teacher, or get in touch with one of her old girls who, perhaps, is out of a job.'

'In case you have to stay on here in this hospital, is there any girl friend who would run down to look after you?'

She shook her head. 'I have a few girl friends,' she replied, 'but the ones I have will be working after tomorrow. No, I haven't anyone who is free to come to Margate.'

Again the expressive gesture of her beautiful, slim hands.

All at once, Ronald made up his mind. He knew that he had fallen deeply in love with this friendless girl, so he determined either to stay on at Margate or return to the town while Heather was laid up.

'I really should be returning to London tomorrow,' he said. 'But when I return to my hotel today I shall phone the manager of my night club and say that I shall stay on in Margate over this week-end.'

'But, but–'

Her voice had a troubled note in it.

He explained, 'My presence really isn't necessary in London every day. Father died six months ago, leaving me a night club and several important businesses, but I have a splendid manager at my club, also a very good secretary. Frankly *they* are the knowledgeable ones and I know that everything will get on well without me, so I'll stay on here and look after you. Regarding my other businesses, I also have splendid managers and other personnel to carry on without me.'

'I ... I ... still don't understand,' she stammered.

'My dear! Don't worry your head about anything, just get well.'

He laid his fingers for a second on the hand that was nearest to him.

Heather felt happy that Ronnie had touched her. Never in her life had she felt so drawn to a man.

Ronald Steele went on, 'I fancy having an extra holiday, also, if you *will* have an explanation, yes, I feel that *someone* ought to be on the spot to help you. It will break the monotony of the day if I come along and chat with you. When I visit I'll bring you anything you need. I'll also do any little commissions for you. To begin with, what about your guest house? I mean, for how long did you book your digs?'

'Till tomorrow morning. I paid in advance.'

'Well! Would you like me to ask the proprietress of Clovelly to pack your things into your suitcase? Then she can let your room.'

'Yes, please. I don't know how to thank you for all you're doing for me.'

'I haven't done anything *yet*. By the way, do call me Ronnie and if I may, I'll call you Heather.'

'All right, Ronnie.'

'Good! Now will I try and get hold of someone who'll put these flowers in water for you?'

'Yes, please, they are so lovely. I would hate them to fade.'

He said, 'I see a nurse coming this way, so I'll ask her.'

The attractive-looking nurse smiled at the young man's request and speedily brought a vase filled with water in which she arranged the flowers.

When the warning bell rang Ronnie got up, but as he bent over Heather he said, 'I promise to come tomorrow. Now what can I bring you? Would you like some candied fruit?'

'Oh, no! Ronnie! You've been far too good to me already. Look at all the things you've brought me today. No! Please just bring *yourself*.'

At the entrance to the Harvey Ward, Ronnie managed to get hold of the Ward Sister.

In answer to the young man's question

Sister replied that it *was* correct that the patient's arm was not broken. 'It's a fracture and the extent of the damage is not yet known, but the patient is to have a thorough check-up tomorrow morning.'

'As Miss Dean has only one relative in the world, namely an uncle and he is in Scotland, may I be allowed to visit her every day?'

'Please come. It will do her good,' the Sister answered.

On the way back to the hotel Ronnie's mind kept dwelling on Heather Dean. She intrigued him. He thought of the look in her eyes when she spoke of her tour with the *corps de ballet*. He wondered why she had not been re-engaged. Something important and damaging professionally must have happened to Heather on this tour, and he wondered what it could have been.

Feeling thirsty Ronnie parked his car and sat down at an open-air café. At a table next to him lounged two long-haired youths and two girls. By the men's clothes he guessed them to be Mods.

As Ronnie drank his tea he saw a man approach the four at the next table.

'I am a reporter,' the newcomer said. 'I understand that you're a Mod? Now, I'd like

42

to know what your attitude is to the Rockers?'

'Oh yeah!' said the younger Mod. 'Well, if you want to know, we *do* like to screw the Rockers. We're out for "kicks". Oh, yeah! I'm going to get me a Rocker's head.'

'Don't take any notice of him,' said the older Mod. 'He's all *"purpled"* up.'

'Do you take the purple heart drug?' asked the reporter.

One of the girls answered.

'Of course we take purple hearts! How else are we to get on? We get kicks all day and have beach parties on the sands all night. If we didn't take purple hearts we couldn't stay awake all night. We Mods-Birds don't want to miss anything.'

As Ronnie looked at the girls' young ravaged faces and their dishevelled hair and crushed clothes he compared them very unfavourably with Heather's calm expression and her beautifully groomed appearance.

The reporter now turned his full attention on the girls.

'Why did you join in all this?' he asked.

The girl, who gave her age as seventeen, answered.

'Because it gives me a thrill, it makes you feel all funny inside. You get butterflies in the stomach and you want the boys to go on and on.'

The reporter indicated the two youths at the table, as he further questioned, 'Are these your special boyfriends? Your *fiancés?*'

The two male Mods gave a rude and disclamatory gesture.

The girl answered, 'We don't have special boyfriends. No, we two girls got a tip what was going to happen so we came down and joined up with a gang of Mods. We'll just stay with them for this week-end and then – who cares anyway!'

The speaker's hair was long and greasy looking. The two girls were dressed in the latest Mod fashion – initialled sweaters, straight very short skirts and 'sneakers'.

'If these boys are not your "steadies" who are they?' persisted the reporter.

'We believe in free love. We don't go in for "one-night stands", but there's nothing wrong in letting a special Mod make love to you. You're not "with it" if you don't.'

'And what about your future?'

'We don't plan for the future. We live for the day.'

'And marriage?'

'Marriage is for grandmas.' The girl gave a shrill laugh. 'We're out for "kicks". If people get in our way, and get hurt, well! It's just too bad.'

Ronnie felt that he couldn't contain himself. He jumped up and turned like a fury on the girl who had been speaking. He seemed to tower over her as he said:

'I've just left a girl of your own age lying badly injured in the Margate hospital. She was knocked over and injured by one of your filthy Mods. The extent of the damage is not yet known, but she may be injured for life, her health and career all ruined because one of your dirty, miserable, mentally unstable hooligans were out for *"kicks"*.'

The two male Mods jumped to their feet. They looked threatening. The reporter gave Ronnie a sympathetic, but a significant look.

So Ronnie turned and went away. He felt that if he stayed he wouldn't have been responsible for his actions.

As he made for the hotel he knew that he had exaggerated Heather's condition. Probably it was his fears for her that had made him do so. He realised that he had fallen in love at first sight with this beautiful little dancer.

After dinner that night Ronnie got on the phone to London. He managed to get through to his manager, William Harcourt.

In reply to Ronnie's question, the manager replied, 'Of course it will be all right if you stay on in Margate. You *did* give me the address of your hotel and the hotel's phone number, so I can get in touch with you, if necessary.'

'Is everything going on all right?'

'Yes, thanks. An unexpected vacancy has occurred in the cabaret. Daisy Ellis – she helps Ali in his conjuring act, you'll remember. Well, she came to me and said that her *fiancé* in New Zealand had sent her the money for her ticket and that she had managed to get a booking to Wellington. Well, all I could do was to wish her luck.'

'What are you doing about this turn, when Daisy goes?'

'Ali Chanderi, the Indian conjurer, says he can temporarily manage to carry on and do his turn unaided. So for the moment I'll just cut out the woman's part in the double turn.'

'That's a pity, because it is an effective and popular part of the double turn.'

'I agree, and I'll look out for a girl to take Daisy Ellis's place.'

A thought came into Ronnie's head and made him say to his manager:

'For the present don't get anyone in Daisy's place.'

'As you say, Mr. Steele!'

After discussing some further business and thanking his manager, Ronnie hung up.

Before Ronnie went to sleep his thoughts again turned on the girl who attracted him so greatly. He reflected that if the worst came to the worst and Heather's injuries prevented her ever dancing again there was a job he could offer her at The Delkushla.

CHAPTER FOUR

The next day the papers were again full of the exploits of the Mods and Rockers during the Bank Holiday period. The battered seaside towns of Brighton and Margate began to count the cost of their Mods and Rockers' Whitsun. The presiding magistrate had given sentences to fifty of the youths who had been arrested and had told them, 'You pollute the air of Margate.' The wife of a doctor in the town had been reported to have said:

'I thoroughly agree with the sentences given by the magistrate. He wants to help the police. These teenagers must be taught a lesson. This town depends on holiday guests, especially people with families. No one will come here when Mods and Rockers batter the town and assault people in this way.'

Now the Mods and Rockers and most of the week-end visitors had departed.

As Ronnie went along the promenade he looked down at the beach and he thought how peaceful everything looked.

He descended the steps and had a swim. Then he sunbathed.

Later on, he did a little shopping as he wanted to take some presents to Heather. First he visited a booksellers and bought papers and a couple of books. As he did so he wondered why he was taking so much trouble for such a recent acquaintance. He couldn't quite answer that question, but he knew that he had been greatly attracted to the young girl from the first, not only on account of her beauty, but because she possessed a sort of 'elusive' charm which greatly interested him. Heather had not made any approaches to him. Since he had become the owner of a night club, as the employer of a number of young and very beautiful women, he had got used to lovely girls throwing themselves at his head. Heather hadn't done so, but he felt that she *did* like him. He noticed that she was almost pathetically grateful for the gifts he brought her. There was, he felt, a mystery, a sense of frustration about the girl's short career as a ballet dancer and he determined to solve the mystery.

When he entered the hospital Heather greeted him warmly and thanked him for his presents.

In answer to his enquiries she answered, 'My bruises must be better because I can turn over in bed now without pain.'

'And your injured arm?'

'As soon as a plaster-cast was put on it I had no more pain. Of course it's inconvenient of a night. I mean, I generally go off to sleep on my left side. Luckily, my right hand is not hurt, so I can write.'

'Have they said anything about the result of your X-ray?'

'No, and I don't like to ask because everyone has been very kind and charming, so I don't want to bother anyone.'

'"Life's a mirror",' he replied. 'I mean, anyone would be nice to you because you are so friendly and sweet.'

'Oh! I don't know about that! My uncle's wife, Aunt Ella, who lives in Scotland, has never liked me, nor approved of my being trained for ballet. She said that I ought to have gone in for a steady profession.'

'I can picture your aunt! That type is unsympathetic to art in any form. Tell me, weren't you happy in the *corps de ballet?*'

'Oh, yes! I was extremely happy when I danced at Monte Carlo and Nice. It was then the spring, and what with the Carnival and the wonderful flowers I just fell in love with the Riviera. I really thought that I was in heaven.'

He nodded sympathetically.

'Yes, I can just imagine the effect the first sight of the Riviera would have on you. But did you enjoy your life as a dancer?'

'Oh, yes! I was ecstatically happy when I danced. On the stage I felt that I had entered another world.'

'I'd like to know more about the feelings and life of a ballet dancer.'

'Well, it is an absorbing life. I was an understudy and when I played Odette in "Swan Lake" at rehearsals or my own part as one of the little swans, I just got so wrapped up in my role that half-an-hour after the conclusion of the ballet I seemed to be still in another world.'

'Is the life of a ballet dancer hard?'

'It is, as I said a minute ago, a life that utterly absorbs. We girls really lived a nun-like existence. On tour we had chaperons who lived with us and guarded the future ballerinas from the local wolves.'

'You were then quite happy on tour?'

'Yes, till...'

She broke off abruptly, the old, frustrated and unhappy look came into her eyes.

51

Ronnie said to himself, 'Yes, I *was* right. Something of a very unhappy nature must have happened to Heather on that Riviera tour. Whatever did happen must have been of a grave nature because it evidently caused the authorities *not* to renew her contract. Yes, she's got some big, and perhaps grim, secret. However, something tells me that one day Heather Dean will tell me what is worrying her.'

But he had to check his thoughts because the girl in the bed was speaking to him.

'For *my* sake,' she said, 'I'm very glad that you are staying on in Margate, but I feel worried, in case your business suffers?'

'Oh, that's all right! To be quite frank – not only my night club, but all my businesses have such splendid managers and managing directors that the firms run without me. I'm not a businessman, my father *was*. I would describe my late Dad as a "financial wizard". The poor dear old boy was very upset when I told him that I didn't want to follow in his footsteps. When I left my public school I begged Dad to let me join my Uncle Charlie who has a farm in Canada.'

'And did you get your way? Tell me what happened.'

'At first Dad utterly refused to let me go to

Canada. He stormed the house down and for days there were scenes galore. Then, finding that I could be neither bullied nor intimidated, he made me a proposition. It was that he would let me go if I promised to return in three years' time. As I was only nineteen at the time, in other words a minor, I felt compelled to give Dad my promise.'

'And did you like Canada?'

'Very much, but when I had been out there two and a half years I got the news that Dad had died suddenly, so I returned to London. I've tried to keep faith with Dad by carrying out his special ideas regarding the night club.'

Heather shook her head. 'I don't understand. Please tell me all about it.'

'Well, Dad was very much against a night club being just a sort of strip-tease joint – a place where men are lured in and made to buy plenty of bad and very expensive liquor. No! Dad's conception, and it's now *mine*, is premises that have lovely and exotic surroundings – a night club where the guests can get well-cooked and reasonably priced food and drink. I have also kept up the standard of the cabaret.'

Ronnie paused.

Heather urged. 'Go on! Tell me more

about the club.'

'Well, in short, I try to give what the advertisement describes as "breathtakingly beautiful and unique oriental surroundings". I cater not only for the man-about-town, but the traveller who wants drink and entertainment late in the evening or early in the morning. I put on a really good cabaret.'

'I know – a number of beautiful blondes?'

'Yes, but there's more to my cabaret than "Les Girls". In fact I have a number of "turns".'

'Such as?'

'A vocalist, a personality dancer, a conjurer and a snake charmer and other turns. I change the programme frequently.'

'Do you have club hostesses?'

'Yes and I see that these girls get a fair deal.'

'What do you mean by that?'

'Well, they get a good salary and their job is solely to act as dance partners. My hostesses do not encourage their partners to order bottle after bottle so that they – the girls, I mean, get a "rake-off".'

'You sound very fair.'

'Well, if employees serve me well I like to treat them well.'

Heather studied her companion. He's got

everything, she thought, good looks, a splendid character, charm, money. He could have any girl. Ronnie could be spending his time with beautiful and talented girls and here he is devoting himself to me.

She said in a reflective tone:

'I can't picture you in a night club. Do you live there?'

'Good Lor' no! I have a service flat in Kensington. Not that I look on that as my home. I'll tell you about the place I love – my *real* home. It is an old manor house in Sussex. Father bought it about ten years ago. It's among the lovely rolling Downs country. The house has a nice bit of ground around it. I'm very fond of Greenham and I'd like to show it to you one day.'

'And I'd love to see it. Does your mother live there?'

'My mother died when I was born. No, the woman who was originally my Nanny is now housekeeper at Greenham. No, I haven't any parents now, and I think you said that your dad and mum were killed in an accident.'

'Yes.' Tears came into Heather's eyes as she spoke. 'It was a strange and terrible accident. One week-end Father and Mother wanted a little jaunt to the sea, so they started off in a motor coach to the coast. It happened when I was sixteen and it was a horrifying affair. I had just left my grammar school and was studying ballet. As I was working that day I couldn't accompany my parents to the sea.'

'What happened?' Ronnie asked.

'As I said a minute ago, my parents had joined a party of day-trippers bound for Brighton. The accident happened at a circular road and on the return journey – when it was all over the survivors told the story. They said that many of the people in the coach had their eyes shut, probably they were pleasurably tired. Well, seven of the people in the coach, including my parents, were killed when a crane-mast – the crane was operating making a new fly-over road – fell on the rear of the coach. I can't tell you the details of the crash because I felt too upset at the time to read the papers.'

Ronnie nodded sympathetically.

'What a terrible shock for you. Also, I expect you were left quite alone to tackle your father's business affairs.'

'Not quite alone. My father's brother, Eric Dean, came up from Edinburgh. His wife couldn't get away and I wasn't sorry because she's a dour, unsympathetic woman.'

'I know the sort. But tell me, however did

you manage for money when your father died?'

'Well, as I said a minute ago, Uncle Eric helped me with the sale.'

'Do you mean the sale of your house?'

'No, it wasn't Father's house. We only rented it. But Uncle helped me with the disposal of some of the furniture and also the sale of china and silver. In this way I had a little sum in hand. Uncle also managed to get me a small flat in Norbury, London. I still live there. About a year after my parents' death I got my first contract and went off on my tour to the Riviera.'

'And after that everything was all right?'

'Oh no!'

Heather's exclamation was involuntary and had a ring of tragedy in it.

For a moment there was a silence. Then Ronnie offered Heather some of the black grapes he had again brought for her.

She smiled her thanks and said:

'*Why* are you so good to me?'

Ronnie shrugged his shoulders.

'Well, to start with I feel a bit responsible for you. I mean, if I had seized you by the arm, taken you to my car and then driven you back to your guest house, well, all this wouldn't have happened.'

'You forget I utterly refused your help.'

'That's true, but, my dear, I'm terribly sorry about your being injured.'

'Yes, but you were not responsible in any way. On the contrary, you helped me tremendously.'

She added, 'I do think it's awful the way those Mods and Rockers have spoilt innocent people's holidays.'

'Yes, and so many people only had the three days at Whitsun.'

'To say nothing of the persons who just came down for the day.'

'How right you are! Oh, Heather, while I think of it, have you any letters for the post?'

She stretched out her hands to her bedside cupboard and took out two envelopes, saying, 'I shall be very grateful if you will post these two notes – one is to a girl friend and the other to the woman who owns my flat.'

'No boy-friends?' he joked.

'At present I'm heart free.'

'What about when you were on the Riviera? Surely you must have had a dark-haired, flashing lover at Monte Carlo or Nice?'

He spoke jokingly and so he was surprised to see a flush spread from the other's neck right up to her forehead.

Seeing that his words had recalled some

unhappy memory he said to himself, 'Something unpleasant and hurtful must have occurred when she was on the Riviera, something to do with a man, something that turned the ballet authorities so much against her that they did not renew her contract.'

He said quickly, 'I just can't imagine how you haven't been snapped up by a man.'

'Perhaps I met the wrong man.' Again a shadow crossed her face.

'Well you have plenty of time. What are your plans? I mean do you dream of becoming a great ballerina?'

To his surprise her eyes filled with tears. She quoted:

'"Some dreams we had".'

At this minute the warning bell rang.

With great reluctance, Ronnie got up and took his departure, first promising Heather to come and see her on the morrow.

On the way out, Ronnie managed to waylay the Ward Sister.

Ronald enquired as to how Heather Dean was getting on.

'Well, since her arm has been in plaster she has been free from pain in her arm and her bruises less painful,' answered the Sister.

'Will Miss Dean be able to leave hospital soon?' asked Ronnie.

59

'As far as I know, the date of her discharge cannot yet be given. It will depend on her rate of progress.'

There was something in the Sister's guarded manner that made Ronnie say:

'Miss Dean has no relatives, at least only an uncle who lives in Scotland. Accordingly, would it be possible for me to have a confidential chat with the doctor in charge of the case?'

'That could be arranged. When are you free?'

'Any day, any time this week.'

The Sister made an appointment to see the doctor in charge of Heather's case, in two days' time.

CHAPTER FIVE

Two days later Ronald Steele found the hospital surgeon helpful and sympathetic.

When Ronnie asked about the result of the X-ray of Heather's arm the medical man remarked:

'Did you know that Miss Dean has also had a thorough check-up?'

'No,' Ronnie answered, 'and as the sole representative of your patient's affairs I shall be deeply grateful for any information. I shall regard what you say as absolutely confidential.'

'Just a minute!'

The surgeon rose and going over to a cabinet, took out an X-ray film and some papers which he studied for a minute or two.

At length the medical man looked up and pronounced:

'Miss Heather Dean is a thoroughly sound and healthy woman. She has recovered quickly from the shock of her accident. Her bruises are much less painful. As I expect you know, she has a badly fractured forearm. I anticipate that will heal but–' He held up the X-ray to the light again. 'There's just one thing.' He studied a form in front of him.

Ronnie waited.

The doctor asked, 'Is it correct that Miss Dean is a ballet dancer?'

'Yes. I understand that at present she is not a member of a ballet corps but is teaching in a school of ballet.'

The doctor shook his head. 'I'm afraid, for all intents and purposes it's the same.'

Once again he studied the X-ray photo.

Ronnie ventured, 'Has Miss Dean sustained any permanent injury?'

'I can't say yet if there is a permanent injury. She must of course keep on the plaster-cast for another few weeks.'

'Does that mean she is to stay on here, in hospital?'

The doctor studied the notes on Heather's case, before replying.

'As the patient has stated that she lives by herself in a flat and consequently has no relative or close friend in her dwelling-place to look after her, I should say that it is absolutely necessary for her to stay in hospital till the plaster-cast is removed.'

Ronnie thought quickly and then said:

'I shall stay on here for a few days and then, although I shall have to return to London, I shall come back to Margate every week-end to see Miss Dean.'

'That's very good of you and I'm sure your thoughtful attention and kindness will go far to help the patient's full recovery.'

The surgeon rose. Ronnie took the hint and also got up.

The doctor asked, 'Would you like to come and see me as soon as the plaster-cast is removed from the patient's arm? I shall then be in a better position to answer your questions regarding Miss Dean.'

After thanking the surgeon, and saying that he would ask for a further appointment as soon as the date of Heather Dean's discharge from hospital was fixed, Ronald Steele left the consulting-room and made his way towards the Harvey Ward.

As usual Heather was delighted to see him. After talking about various things Ronnie asked, 'Does the proprietress of Clovelly smoke?'

'Yes?' There was a note of interrogation in the monosyllable.

Ronnie explained: 'Good! Because the owner of your guest house was good to you, so I want to give her a little present before I leave Margate.'

A look of disappointment came into Heather's eyes.

'*Are* you leaving Margate?' she asked.

'Only temporarily, dear. I shall run up to London on Saturday afternoon, that is after I have made my usual visit to you. However, I shall return to this town on Friday night and stay for the week-end. You see, my dear, I've just had a chat with the surgeon in charge of your case and he has told me that while your arm is in plaster it is best for you to stay here. I feel I must spend five days a week looking after my night club and other businesses, but I promise to come down every week-end.'

'How good you are to me!'

'I've done nothing, but I want you to promise to do something for me.'

'I'll love to do anything for you, Ronnie, that is if I can. What is it?'

He held out a closed envelope on which he had written her name.

'To make me happy, please accept the few banknotes which you'll find in this envelope.'

Noticing the expression on her face he went on. 'Treat the money as a loan if you like, but please accept it. You see, the thought of going away to London and leaving you here without any or little money, well, it's worrying me to death.'

'But I haven't any expenses in hospital.'

'Maybe! But you may fancy some fruit or a bottle of barley water or lime juice cordial, or in fact anything. You said the other day that some of the patients are allowed out for a short period, well, I'm sure that any such persons or a nurse or a ward maid would buy anything you require. Now dear, put the notes away in safety and don't say another word about this little sum.'

Later on when Ronald Steele left the hospital he drove to a tobacconist. Here he bought a box of one hundred cigarettes. He re-entered his car and driving to Clovelly he presented the box to the proprietress.

He explained, 'I shall be so pleased if you will accept the box of cigarettes. You have been so kind to Miss Dean.'

'I did nothing, Mr. Steele, but if there is anything I can do for your friend, I'll love to do it.'

'Well, as a matter of fact I would be very grateful if you could help me in one little matter.'

The woman waited so Ronald went on.

'*You* packed Miss Dean's clothes so you

are in a position to answer my question. It's only this: do you think Miss Dean has brought down enough clothes for several weeks? I know she only anticipated staying for the Bank Holiday week-end.'

The proprietress thought for a minute and then volunteered the information, 'As your friend has to stay in bed she won't want anything in the day-dress line, but she only brought down one nightdress.'

Ronnie took out a wallet which held banknotes. He said, 'I shall be very grateful if you will buy me two nightdresses such as a dainty and attractive woman like yourself would wear. Now, is there anything else you could suggest?'

The proprietress warmed to her task, because she was falling under the spell of Ronnie's good looks and charming manner.

'Your friend brought down a lovely housecoat; but if I see a pretty bed-jacket will I get it?'

'Please *do*. You *are* being helpful – can you think of other things?'

'Yes, additional handkerchiefs and vests.'

Ronnie took out a bundle of one and five-pound notes.

'Please give me a rough idea of the cost,' he began, 'and I'll give it to you. I'm deeply grateful to you.'

As Ronald Steele left, the smiling landlady of Clovelly she said:

'Call this time tomorrow and I'll have the parcel containing your friend's clothes ready for you.'

As Ronnie left for his hotel he reflected that he would leave these things for Heather on his way up to London.

CHAPTER SIX

On Saturday after Ronald left The Denham he lost no time in leaving Margate and heading for town.

On arriving in London, Ronnie was soon on his way to The Delkushla. On arriving there he went straight to his manager's office.

Mr. Harcourt got out a bottle of whisky, a siphon and two glasses. At the same time the manager asked, 'Shall I phone through to the restaurant and have a meal sent along to your room?'

'No, thanks. I'll eat later. Now, I expect you'd like my signature for letters and cheques?'

'Yes, please.'

When they had finished their business Ronnie said:

'Now I'll go to my room to look through my private letters that have arrived for me. After that I'll pop along to the restaurant.'

Mr. Harcourt saw his employer to the door. In the passage was lounging a handsome, young Indian. He greeted Ronald Steele warmly and the owner of the club returned the greeting with equal warmth, because Ronnie and the conjurer, Ali Chanderi, had been friends at the same public school and when Ronnie had gone to Canada the two young men had corresponded.

Ronnie said, 'I guess you're waiting to speak to me.'

'Yes, please, I won't keep you long.'

Chanderi threw open the door of his own room which was nearby. Ronnie entered and sat down. For a little while, the men chatted about the behaviour of the Mods and Rockers at Margate.

Ronnie asked, 'Has everything gone all right here?'

'Yes, with the exception of my partner packing up my act by sailing for New Zealand.'

'Don't worry, Ali! I hear you've managed all right alone.'

'Oh, I've carried on with my conjuring, but may we have a replacement for Daisy? The "double turn" is too good to drop.'

'Oh, we won't do that! Yes, it *is* a good turn, and it's you who created it! I'll see that you get a replacement for Daisy within a short period. Will that do?'

'Nicely thanks!'

Ali rose, went to a cupboard and came back with a bottle and glasses saying:

'You *will* have a drink, won't you?'

Ronnie laughed. 'I *shouldn't* really drink on an empty stomach,' he protested.

'Oh, just one!'

Ronnie didn't like to offend his employee, but he felt it wasn't wise to mix drinks in this way.

Later on, when Ronald got up to leave, Ali warned him, 'I saw Carmen waiting outside your room.'

'She can't get in. There are only two keys to my door, I have one and Mr. Harcourt has the other.'

'She told me that she was waiting to speak to you. It seems that someone she knows saw you go into Mr. Harcourt's room.'

'Don't worry! If she *is* hanging about I'll soon get rid of her.'

The Indian persisted, 'She's mad on you.'

'Oh, Carmen is always going "bonkers" over some man!'

'You're right there! She's a bad woman – worse than any prostitute. She's already had *affaires* with two married men and has taken these fellows from their wives. Carmen will do her best to make you mad about her and have an *affaire* with her. Then she'll try to rush you into a marriage with her, saying that you are the father of her child-to-be.'

Ronnie threw his head back and laughed. 'You're a loyal pal,' he said, 'but don't worry about me. Nothing is farther from my thoughts than having an *affaire* with our sultry Spaniard – nothing. To tell you the truth, and in deepest confidence, I met my fate during my stay at Margate. She's the loveliest and most attractive girl in the world. You must meet her, Ali. However, I can't tell you about her now because it's getting late and I haven't yet been to my room. I'll take a safe bet that there are "aeons" of letters waiting for me on my desk.'

'Yes, and you may have to deal with Carmen if she's still hanging about your room.'

'Oh! I'll soon settle her.'

With a farewell grin Ronnie left Ali and made for his office. He entered and walked over to the desk and examined the pile of letters lying there.

As Ali had predicted, he had scarcely sat down when there was a tap on the door followed by the entrance of the person who knocked. It was Carmen. She walked across the room and settled herself in the most

71

comfortable chair. Ronnie held a hand up at her entrance. He did not welcome Carmen, neither did he sit down. He just towered over the Spanish girl and glared at her as he demanded, 'What in the hell do you mean coming, uninvited, into my room? What do you want? Say what you've come to say and clear out!'

As he spoke he studied the Spanish girl. She was as astonishingly dark-haired as was Heather, but there the likeness ended because Carmen, through her self-indulgence and strong passions, had let her looks and figure go to seed.

'I've come to welcome you back,' she announced.

'Very nice of you, I'm sure.' There was a sarcastic note in Ronnie's voice, 'but it's very late, and I have a lot to do. I've been so pressed for time that I haven't had anything substantial to eat all day.'

'Poor dear. Let's go along to the restaurant now.'

'That's impossible!' he waved his hand towards the desk and the pile of correspondence that awaited him.

'Please leave at once,' he ordered.

'All right! But Ronnie,' she got up, but moved very close to him, 'I'll go, but *do* stay here tonight. You've got a bedroom here,' she jerked her head towards the adjoining room. 'Well, I can bide till everyone has left The Delkushla and then I'll sneak in here.'

Carmen put her arms around his neck and moved close to him, kissing him passionately.

Ronnie disengaged himself quickly. Carmen persisted, 'I'm mad about you. I'll have to go now I know, but I'll return when the coast is clear and then...' Her eyes expressed what her lips had left unsaid.

Her companion grinned, and taking Carmen by the shoulders he walked her across the room.

Before he opened the door he said:

'You ask what I'm going to do tonight. Well, I'm going to my flat as I always do, of course.'

'But I'm mad on you. If you'll only return, my love, I could make you and myself very happy.'

Ronnie gave a gesture of amazement. 'Carmen, you really *are* going ga-ga! Can't you get it into your head that I have no idea of having an *affaire* with you.'

'Why, Ronnie?'

'For one reason I have neither the time nor the inclination. Now *will* you go?'

As she didn't move and seemed quite unconvinced Ronnie said unwisely, 'Also, I have got a lovely girl. I don't want anyone but Heather.'

The moment he had spoken Ronnie regretted having mentioned the name of the girl he loved. He realised that the drinks he had had on an empty stomach had made him mentally tired and incautious. He now deeply regretted having mentioned Heather Dean's name.

Carmen's mouth hardened. An angry look came into her eyes. She repeated, 'Heather! I'll remember that name. I'll do my best to come between you. I'll see that she doesn't get you.'

Ronnie opened the door and gently pushed Carmen through the entrance, saying:

'Don't talk such tripe! Really you'll end up as a "nut-case". Now 'op it! I have aeons and aeons of work to do.'

Ronnie closed and locked the door after Carmen. Then going over to his desk he sat down and started dealing with his correspondence.

When Ronald had finished his letters he thought he would make for the restaurant. Accordingly he went downstairs and had a meal.

When he had finished he came into the main dancing hall. He stood there studying the scene and wondering how the whole club would strike Heather when he brought her to it. So he first stood in a quiet spot where he had an excellent view of the largest room. Later on he went upstairs, all the time imagining how the place would appear to Heather.

The late Mr. Steele had spent a great amount of money on the 'décor' of The Delkushla. He wished to attract visitors from the Continent, from the Commonwealth and from America. Accordingly, he got hold of a first-class decorator who succeeded in creating beautiful and arresting-looking rooms. Ronald's father appealed to the family instinct of the overseas visitors by keeping his cabaret absolutely free from any suggestiveness. In this way the most important English and international touring companies frequently brought parties to the Delkushla.

When visitors entered the club dance-hall on a hot summer evening they were instantly struck by the deliciously cool appearance of the dance-hall. It was a large, long and very lofty hall. It really consisted of two rooms because upstairs there was a balcony which ran all around the hall and on which were placed little tables and chairs. Here refreshments were served, so the club guests could eat and drink and watch the dancing at the same time. They also had a good view of the cabaret when it started.

Running parallel to the wall of the balcony was a wall of matchwood in which were several doors. These led to a long corridor. Opening off this corridor were the rooms of the owner of the club, the manager and top-ranking members of the staff. Here, too, were the rooms of the solo turns – Carmen Nevada, Ali Chanderi and others. The group turns like the Lovelies had a large dressing-room at the back of the stage. The club guests never went through the doors in the matchboard partition, because they knew that this part of the club was private. Also, it was a commodious club and consisted of several beautiful and comfortable rooms. The décor, the service, the excellent food and wines and the interesting and varied turns of the Cabaret all exemplified the club's name Delkushla, which in English meant 'Heart's Delight'.

The large dance-hall was particularly eastern in character. The walls and pillars were of marble, the hangings and curtains of exquisite Indian silk. Over the doors were oriental bead curtains whose eastern character was accentuated by the musical hanging bells that jangled as the members went through the doorways.

A beautiful fountain, where coloured lights played on the water, was in the middle of the hall. The drop scene on the stage was a well-painted representation of the beautiful Taj-Mahal, on whose walls the founder had inscribed 'If there is a Paradise on Earth – it is this! it is this!' Dancing took place in the centre of the large room. Around the dance-hall were grouped little tables on which refreshments were served.

At the far end of the hall, opposite the stage, was a bar and doors to the restaurant and dining-room opened off the main hall.

When his tour of his club was finished Ronald felt suddenly weary so, after saying 'Good night' to his manager, he left The Delkushla and drove to his service flat.

CHAPTER SEVEN

In hospital Heather found that the life she was leading was of a type of dream-like existence. She knew that it was the entrance of Ronald Steele into her life that had given it this happy trance-like quality. Previous to her visit to Margate the word 'man' and 'lover' had been synonymous with the nightmare events that had occurred at Nice, and with disgrace and a broken career. After her tour in the *corps de ballet* Heather had vowed that she would never again even get friendly with a man. Now everything was changed and she knew that she was hopelessly and irrevocably in love with Ronald Steele.

Ronnie was never absent from her thoughts. All the morning she looked forward to his afternoon visit. After he had left, Heather spent all the evening fondly looking at and examining the presents that he had brought her and recalling all that Ronnie had said during his visit. The young girl went off to sleep thinking of the man she loved and woke up the next morning imagining what she would say to Ronnie when he called at the hospital after lunch.

Apart from the disability of a heavy plaster-cast on her arm and having to stay in bed, Heather Dean found life quite pleasant at the Emsham Hospital. She thought the food was very good and it was brought to her on her movable bed-tray. The young girl was so grateful and pleasant to the nurses that she became a favourite with the staff. The patients also liked the beautiful young ballerina. She became very friendly with her immediate neighbours.

The woman in the next bed was a widow, a Mrs. Fay, who had been a nurse. As this patient was able to get about she frequently came and sat in a chair by the other's bedside. Here Mrs. Fay criticised the ward in general and, in particular, the morals and 'goings on' of a nice-looking blonde named Lynne aged twenty, who occupied the opposite bed.

The ex-ballerina found Mrs. Fay rather a scandalmonger. The widow's scathing criticism was particularly directed at the diaphanous garments which Lynne wore not only in the ward but in the garden. Lynne was usually accompanied by a small, brown-haired Cockney girl, Stella, who occupied a bed near Heather. This Cockney child also floated about in the most revealing nightdresses and negligées.

That morning, when the two girls had left the ward to go into the garden, Mrs. Fay got out of bed and came and sat by Heather's bedside.

The widow jerked her head towards the retreating figures of the two girls.

'Do you know where those two are going?' she demanded.

'To sit on the veranda to get the sun.'

Mrs. Fay gave a disdainful laugh.

'To get the *sun* may be the right answer,' she replied, 'but you spell it with an "o". Don't you believe it that those two girls are sitting on the verandah. No, that Lynne makes for the seats around the corner and at the far end of the garden.'

'Why does Lynne go there?'

'Because those seats are outside the men's ward, and the fellows come out and sit beside her – men often old enough to be her father.'

'And Stella?'

'Oh, Lynne drags the kid along as a blind to what she's doing! Stella has no right to even be in this ward because she's only fourteen.'

'Why isn't she in the children's ward?'

'I heard that the juvenile part of the hospital is full. Also, both girls are leaving tomorrow.'

'I'm glad of that. I mean, for Stella's sake I'm glad that she'll have a mother's love and care again.'

'Mother's care and protection! Don't make me laugh! Have you seen the made-up, dyed, addled-looking specimen who calls herself Stella's mother?'

Heather shook her head.

'Well,' went on Mrs. Fay, 'I think Stella has no one to look after her and is probably running the streets at all hours of the day and night. If you ask me, Stella is very knowledgeable sexually.'

That evening something occurred which proved the accurateness of Mrs. Fay's criticism.

As Heather was eating her supper she started thinking about Ronnie's return to London and the coming weekend. All at once she longed to speak to him.

When Heather saw a member of the staff coming towards the bed with the intention of taking away the supper tray, she said:

'Nurse, I'm so sorry to trouble you but do you think it would be possible for me to ring

up my man-friend? I've just remembered
that as he is returning to London this week-
end there is something I specially want to
say to him.'

The nurse liked Heather.

'I'll get you the telephone at once,' she
replied. 'That is, if no one else is using it.'

The older woman returned in a few
minutes' time pushing the table containing
the movable telephone.

After plugging in, Nurse Adams offered:

'If you give me the money and your
friend's telephone number I'll dial for you.'

In a short while the nurse handed the girl
the receiver saying, 'You're through. I'll be
back in a few minutes to take back the
phone.'

It was a joy to Heather to hear the man she
loved and, as she had anticipated, he was
only too eager to do any little commission
for her.

After a short conversation Heather asked,
'Have you had your dinner, dear?'

Ronnie laughed and answered, 'I was just
sitting down to eat it when I was told that a
lady wanted me on the phone.'

'Oh, you poor darling, you must be
starving. I'll ring off at once.'

In a short space of time she had done so.

As she was replacing the receiver she felt a little hot hand grabbing hers. It was Stella. In her other hand the girl held out a sixpence, saying:

'Quick, Heather, I want to make a call before that old cat of a Nurse Adams comes back for the phone.'

'I'm afraid I may overhear what you say but, as you know, I can't move out of bed.'

'That's okay, you're my Buddy! I don't mind you hearing what I say.'

The Cockney dialled the operator and said, 'I'm in hospital and I've only got a sixpence. Will you dial this number for me?'

Heather next heard, 'Is that you, Len? Oh, boy, it's the tops! I'm leaving hospital tomorrow.' ... 'Oh, yeah! I *should* say! Same time, same place tomorrow night.' ... 'Well! in some ways I'll miss this dump. I and my pal Lynne we don't 'alf get up to some larks here. This morning Lynne and I spent all the time round the corner of the garden in the men's part. Two blokes and Lynne and I played "Consequences". One of the men started a *Nature* programme and, oh boy, was my face red at some of the things the blokes said!'... 'Oh, Len! It's not fair to carry on like that. They were only *old* blokes and I'll never see them again. You're my steady.'

Evidently Len was not to be placated because Stella started a flow of endearments, evidently to make up for her participation in the 'Nature' programme.

'Oh, Len! Fancy you being jealous! Why you're my light and my delight...' Stella's voice droned on. Heather smiled to herself because she knew the Cockney was repeating what an American girl said about one of the Beatles in a radio broadcast over the air about an hour ago.

'Yes, Len, you're fab! You thrill me! You...'

'Stella!' Nurse Adams pounced. 'Stella, hang up at once! I gave *you* no permission to phone. Replace that receiver at once!'

'Oh! 'orlright.'

After a farewell word of endearment Stella retreated to her bed in a furious temper.

Nurse Adams explained, 'I want the phone for Mrs. Richardson. She wants to catch her husband before he goes on night duty. Mrs. Richardson is leaving hospital tomorrow and wishes to ask her husband to bring along her clothes.'

When the nurse had departed, trundling the table with the phone on it, Stella returned to Heather's bedside.

'Poisonous old cat!' She jerked her head towards Nurse Adams' retreating form.

'The old swine's got a down on me.'

'No she hasn't, Stella, and besides nothing matters to you now. I mean, you're leaving tomorrow. Have some of my chocolates while I tell you something I think funny. This afternoon at visiting time the patient, who left to spend a week in a convalescent home, came in.'

Stella just nodded. Her mouth was too full of chocolates to utter a sound.

'Well, this ex-patient said that there was a marvellous old lady aged ninety-eight in the home, whose hearing and sight, in fact everything is perfect. Well, this patient, (I mean the old lady of ninety-eight), walked out of the nursing home yesterday saying that "it was a boring place and she was going somewhere where she could get some excitement".'

Stella did not laugh. She repeated:

'That Nurse Adams always had a down on me. Do you know, the first night I was here, well I must have got to sleep about nine. Well, I think it was about an hour later when, Gor blimey, she wakes me up to give me a *sleeping* pill. She's a "nut-case" if you ask me.'

Heather laughed, but late that night she recalled Stella's words because very much the same thing occurred to her.

By half-past nine the ballerina had fallen asleep.

About an hour later she awoke with a start to find that one of the lights had been switched on. In addition two figures stood by her bed. One person she recognised as the night nurse. The other was an extremely neat little figure. The newcomer said:

'I am the Night Sister. I have just returned to hospital after a holiday.'

As Heather remained silent the Night Sister added, what the girl later discovered was a formula:

'And how are you?'

Heather would have liked to say many things. Her actual reply was, 'I'm getting on nicely, Sister.'

'Good! I hope you'll get off to sleep soon.'

The young girl felt like replying, 'I *was* asleep.' However she just smiled.

The Sister continued her tour of the ward.

Heather could see the dapper little figure stopping at each bed and always using the same words to every patient, 'And how are you?'

Suddenly the monotony of the dialogue was interrupted by a thin, answering voice. It came from the old lady in the corner bed.

'It's a pity, my dear' – the patient addressed the Night Sister in almost patronising tones, 'It's a pity, my dear, you haven't something better to do than going traipsing about the ward in the dead of night waking the poor patients from their sleep.'

Quite unruffled the neat little figure, accompanied by the night nurse went on inspecting the various patients.

Heather had raised herself on her elbow and was watching the Night Sister's progress. Now the small, slight, blue-clad figure was at the bed of the mentally deranged patient whom the patients had dubbed:

'My-poor-leg woman.'

Nurse Adams had discussed this patient with Heather. The first time the girl had heard this patient scream she had asked the nurse:

'Is that patient opposite in great pain with her leg?'

Nurse Adams had answered, 'No, she hasn't any pain at all. She had a fall and bruised her leg and she's got a phobia that she's in great pain. She screams before anyone touches her leg.'

So now Heather, like all the other patients, awaited with interest the reception 'My-poor-leg woman' was going to give the superbly confident, dapper little Night Sister.

Heather could see the two uniformed figures stopping at the mentally-deranged patient's bed and the Sister's usual formula chiming out:

'And how are you?'

The patient in the bed almost opposite Heather said in deceptively mild tones, 'Could you help me sit up in bed?'

Night Sister fell into the trap. She signalled the nurse to help at the other side and in an efficient way she put her arm around the woman and assisted her to a sitting position.

Instantly the ward rang with piercing cries.

'Oh, my poor leg! Oh, my poor leg! You cruel woman, you've hurt my leg! Oh, my poor leg! Oh, my poor leg!'

Heather fancied that the Night Sister quickened her pace as she finished visiting the last few beds. The girl watched the Sister going out of the door. Instantly the 'My-poor-leg woman' ceased her cries. The light was extinguished and Heather was not long getting off to sleep and she slept on till the morning.

CHAPTER EIGHT

During the weeks that followed Heather lived for the week-ends because they brought the visits of the man she loved.

Heather's last visit in the hospital was a particularly happy and exciting one for the girl because early on the Thursday morning she was taken in a movable chair to the X-ray room.

Later in the day she was again transported from the Harvey Ward this time to the room of the surgeon in charge of her case.

When she opened the door she saw that the Sister of Harvey Ward was also present. They were looking at an X-ray photo; which, on her entrance, the surgeon held out to her, saying:

'Your picture is a good one. Look, you're all in one piece.'

He motioned to the Ward Sister, who, with her special scissors and cutter, quickly and deftly removed the plaster-cast and bandages.

The surgeon smiled at Heather and

jerking his head towards the plaster-cast that now lay on the table, said:

'You're pleased to get rid of that, aren't you?'

'I'm terrifically glad and thank you very much.'

Gently and skilfully the surgeon examined Heather's arm. Next he asked her to do certain movements with it.

'Now put your right hand above your head.'

She tried and grimaced.

'You're a bit stiff.' There was a kind and an encouraging note in the surgeon's voice. He went on:

'You will have to have physiotherapy treatment.'

He explained that in her case it would mean having heat treatment and doing light exercises. 'I shall see that the notes of your case are immediately forwarded to your own doctor in London,' he said.

Heather returned to her ward with a thankful heart. She thought what a surprise Ronnie would get on the morrow when he saw her out of bed and wearing a pretty dress.

Next day Ronnie motored down from London in the morning. He dropped his small suitcase at the Denham Hotel and from there he phoned the hospital because he wanted to ascertain the time of his appointment with Heather's surgeon. Ronald was asked to call at half-past two that day.

As the clock struck the half-hour Ronnie was shown into the medical man's room.

Ronald found the doctor the soul of courtesy.

In answer to the young man's enquiry, 'How is Miss Dean?' the surgeon replied:

'Yesterday she had an X-ray for her forearm. It was satisfactory, namely we found that the bone is all in one piece. I have recommended a course of physiotherapy treatment – she has had this yesterday and this morning.'

As Ronald looked puzzled the doctor explained: 'The rays of a heat-lamp have been turned on the patient's forearm and she has been given light exercises. When she returns to London her own doctor will arrange for similar treatment.'

'Does this mean that Miss Dean is now absolutely all right?'

The surgeon shook his head and in medical jargon started explaining the case.

All Ronnie could understand was the

phrase 'strained ligaments'.

He shook his head and said to the surgeon, 'I'm very sorry, but I don't understand medical terms. Could you be so very kind as to explain the case to me just in the simplest language of a layman.'

The surgeon replied with a question, 'Did you say that the patient is a ballerina?'

'Yes. At present she is not in a *corps de ballet* but teaches dancing in a school of ballet.'

'For this question, teaching in a school of ballet or dancing is very much the same thing. I'm afraid I have to tell you that it is very unlikely that the patient will ever be able to dance or teach dancing again.'

'And if she *does* go back to teach in that school of ballet?'

'She may damage herself permanently. At present her arms and legs are utterly incapable of the strenuous limbering-up exercises of the ballet.'

Ronnie raised hot, angry eyes to those of the surgeons.

'It is *tragic!*' he exclaimed, 'that a young girl's life should be ruined through the action of a vicious young hooligan. After all, the girl, who incidentally is practically penniless, will be prevented from earning her own living.'

'Only as a dancer, or as a teacher in a school of ballet,' corrected the doctor. 'In an ordinary job, or as a housewife she will be able to lead a normal and perfectly healthy life. Incidentally, are you able to identify her attacker? Because if so, I understand she can claim compensation.'

Ronnie shook his head. 'I was, I think, the only witness of the incident. Miss Dean's attacker raced off at top speed. I attended the magistrate's court next day, and I could not spot the fellow among the accused.'

'In that case the only thing for the girl to do is to claim the ordinary sick leave allowance when she returns to London.'

'Is Miss Dean to be discharged soon from hospital?'

'Yes, she can leave here on Saturday. She has given us the name and address of her health doctor in London. We shall impress on her the necessity of visiting her medical man and to continue with her treatment.'

'Thank you. May I ask a great favour?'

'And that is?'

'Is it necessary to tell Miss Dean *now* that she will never dance again?'

'At present it is not necessary, and I have no intention of doing so. The revelation can come later from her London doctor. He will choose the right moment to give her the information.'

Ronald thanked the medical man and as it was now visiting time he made his way to the Harvey Ward. Heather was sitting in a chair and proudly showed him her arm free from the plaster-cast. Ronnie disclosed to her the fact that she was to leave hospital on Saturday. He added that he had seen the hospital surgeon.

'May I run you back to London in my car?' he offered.

'Thank you so much, Mr. Steele.'

'Mister, to you!' he joked.

'All right, Ronnie!'

'That's better, Heather.'

They both laughed.

Heather said, 'I ought to write to Madame Eglantine to say that I'll be back at her school on Monday.'

'Don't write any such thing, my dear. As I told you, I had a talk to the house surgeon here about you. He said that, although you were a very healthy girl and had got on well, you need to rest when you get back to London. Accordingly, he is going to give you a medical certificate which will enable you to draw a sick-pay allowance. When this certificate has expired you must visit your own doctor in London.'

'Everyone is being very kind to me, especially *you*, Ronnie.'

'I haven't done anything, but next week we must have some little jaunt.'

'That would be lovely.'

'Do you know if your special nurse here eats sweets?'

'Yes, I gave her some of the chocolates you brought me.'

'Good! I'll bring her a box of chocolates and you give it to her when you leave. I'll bring two large boxes. The second one the other nurses can share between them.'

'I don't know why you are so good to me.'

'*You're* not getting the boxes of chocolates,' he joked. 'But, Heather, if you want to please me, promise me one thing.'

'What do you want me to promise?'

'To go *regularly* to your doctor when you return to London and to persevere with any treatment he recommends.'

'I promise!'

'Good girl! And if you are ever worried about anything remember I'm always at the other end of the telephone.'

Heather's eyes filled with tears. 'I'm so glad that I came to Margate,' she exclaimed.

'My sweet, you must be going ga-ga! If you had only gone to another holiday resort you might not have had this bad accident.'

'Yes, but if I had gone elsewhere I might have never met you.'

Ronnie saw the deep affection in the girl's eyes and he was glad. He simply said, 'There's the warning bell, so I must go. You see, I have to find out when I'm to call in my car for you tomorrow.'

The hospital authorities asked Ronald to call for Heather at one o'clock on the Saturday. They had volunteered the information that the patient would be given her lunch at twelve o'clock.

As Ronnie disliked a hurried lunch he left the hotel before the meal started. He had sandwiches and drinks at a saloon bar on the way to the hospital.

He put Heather and her luggage into the car.

A nurse had accompanied the girl to the door and she wished her ex-patient the best of everything. The woman turned to Ronnie and smiled as she remarked, 'Miss Dean deserves the best of luck because she's behaved like a first-class little trooper.'

As the car left the building the pleasant nurse waved; so did several patients who

96

had come to the windows of the hospital.

On their journey up to London, Ronnie stopped at a charming little restaurant where they had an early tea.

As they were approaching their destination Ronnie asked:

'Are you feeling very tired?'

'Not at all. You are a splendid driver. It was good of you to give me a lift back. I love your car. It's so elegant-looking and very comfortable.'

'Well, come out in it tomorrow.'

Heather's face expressed her pleasure.

'It's very good of you.'

'All right! What time shall I call for you in the morning – eleven?'

Heather shook her head.

'I have already taken up far too much of your time and you're sure to have a lot to do now that you're back in London.'

'Not of a Sunday.'

'But you have your club to see to. So, no! I won't meet you in the *morning*, but I'd love to go out with you in the afternoon.'

'All right! I'll call for you at three. Now I don't know where your road is, so I'll have to ask you to direct me.'

When they drove up to a villa in Norbury the occupant of the house evidently heard them coming and came down the garden path. Heather explained to Ronnie in a whisper that she had sent her landlady a card giving a rough idea when she would return.

Mrs. Spence greeted the girl warmly.

'I was so sorry to hear about your accident. How are you?' she said.

'I'm feeling much better, thanks. May I introduce Mr. Steele.'

After a minute's conversation Ronnie said to Heather, 'I'll get your luggage out of the boot.'

When he had got Heather's suitcase Ronnie followed the two women up the garden path.

Mrs. Spence invited him in.

He declined. 'It's very good of you, but I must go along to a club I own. Now, will I carry Miss Dean's case to her room?'

'No, thanks, Mr. Steele, my husband has come home, so he'll see to that.'

A minute later Ronald drove off, having first reminded Heather that he was calling for her at three the next day.

CHAPTER NINE

The week following her return to London was a time of great happiness for Heather Dean. Ronnie spared no expense in entertaining her. Only pressing business took him from her side. He wanted to give her a good time, not only because he loved her, but because of his compassion. He felt deeply sorry that her chance of, perhaps, one day becoming a famous ballerina had been ruined by the act of one of the juvenile delinquents who had ruined so many persons' Bank Holiday. Also it was evidently the second time that her career had been interfered with by someone's criminal or negligent deed. Ronnie often speculated as to what *had* happened to Heather at Nice, and he wondered if he would ever learn her secret. As the hospital doctor had given Heather a medical certificate for sick absence she had no reason yet to immediately visit her London doctor. Consequently, she did not yet know that she was forbidden to return to Madame Eglantine's

Ballet School. As she had been told at The Emsham that she need not always wear the sling on her arm, she dispensed with it when she went out with Ronald Steele.

Ronnie was glad that Heather's London doctor was a Fellow of the Royal College of Surgeons because he felt that the woman he loved would get the best of surgical treatment from the man who was on paper a G.P. but by his qualifications he could have been a specialist. When Heather visited Dr. West, F.R.C.S., Ronald Steele wondered what the surgeon's decision would be. Meantime he decided to take advantage of the lovely weather and give the girl a really good time.

Although Ronald Steele made no pretensions to be the acute business man his father was, he did his duty by his managing directors by putting in an appearance when they required it of him. Consequently he was not always free in the day-time. On such an occasion when he had been busy all day and the Delkushla didn't require his presence that evening he took Heather to the Mermaid Theatre. She had never been there before so when she found that their seats were in the front row she gave a little exclamation of delight.

'Oh, Ronnie, isn't it lovely! Why we are only a few yards from the stage.'

It was a Restoration comedy, which Heather enjoyed intensely. Ronnie caught the infection of her happiness.

Now that her general health was restored she just lived every moment of her existence. Ronnie felt that with Heather it was just good to be alive.

At the conclusion of the play they had supper in the building.

As they entered the restaurant he asked, 'Would you like to sit where you can watch the river?'

'Yes, please.'

The food was excellent and the river traffic made an enchanting panorama in front of their eyes as they ate.

One of the attendant's eyes were caught by the superlatively happy face of the brunette. Accordingly the waiter brought a large royal-blue souvenir of the menu card with a picture of a mermaid on the outside.

The attendant presented Heather with the large royal-blue card saying:

'Perhaps Madam would like a menu card as souvenir of this evening.'

'Thank you very much. I have thoroughly enjoyed my visit to the Mermaid.'

The next day as Ronnie was free he called in his car for Heather and ran her down to Richmond.

He parked near the green and then showed her the old houses where the original Maids of Honour lived.

'Now I'll point out the only remains of Richmond Palace, famous in Tudor times,' he said.

'Is there much left of the Palace?'

'Nothing only a wall. Come along and I'll show you.'

Later they had lunch at the Maids of Honour Restaurant. After their meal Ronnie bought Heather a box of famous 'Maids of Honour' pastries.

They took the turning by the restaurant to the river. As they passed a boat-house an idea struck Ronnie.

'Would you like a row on the river?'

'I'd love it.'

As the sun was shining they spent a happy time on the water. Later they tied up, and lazed under the shade of a tree.

Because his presence was needed at the Delkushla that evening he had to run Heather back home after an early tea.

At the club that night, Mr. Harcourt again reminded his employer of the necessity of getting a replacement for Daisy, the snake-charmer.

Next day, as it was a fine morning and Ronnie was free, he phoned Heather and said that he would call for her at eleven.

They took a train to Kingston-on-Thames where they got out and walked into the town because Ronnie wanted to show her the ancient stone where the Anglo-Saxon kings had been crowned. They found this coronation stone near the market place just off the square where the statue of Queen Elizabeth I stands to commemorate her connection with Kingston.

As it was such a lovely day, they walked from Kingston to Hampton Court across the Home Park. Here they entered the court by a wild part of the Gardens where the water-lily leaves were so thick upon the stream as to almost conceal the water. Flowers grew naturally in the long grass making a glorious patch of colour.

They walked to the Palace gardens.

'Let's watch the fountains play.' Heather pointed as she said this.

They stood for a while admiring the cascade of water.

After that they crossed the Broad Walk, with the herbaceous border on one side, and they came to the old Tudor tennis courts. Four people were having a game. They watched till the set was finished.

They came out into the sunlight.

'I must show you the giant vine now,' Ronnie said.

They walked by the hall where once oranges had been grown.

In the garden by the Orangery were few visitors, so they sat on a seat in the sunshine, content and happy.

After a while Ronnie got up and pulled Heather to her feet, saying:

'Let's go and see the Mantagna Pictures.'

They admired the historical portraits in the big garden-room near the Orangery. Then they made their way around to the front of the Palace. As they walked the beauty of the day seemed to close around them. Amongst the trees they marvelled at the black-and-white of the magpie and they smiled at the harsh chatter of his anger. They caught the swift beauty of an occasional redwing flying low over the gardens. Along the well-tended flower beds and by the trim lawns they strolled entranced, admiring the balanced order of Wren's architecture.

'What a good guide you are, Ronnie!'

'Don't speak too soon, Heather,' he

laughingly replied. 'I may lose you yet. Wait till we've got through the Maze before you boast about me being a good guide.'

On the way to the glasshouses they admired the sweet-smelling Tudor Knot Gardens on their right, while on their left was the Dutch Garden with its bright but prim beauty.

They wandered on, charmed with the fountains and the gardens – the sweep of lawns seen through arches of dark trees and edged with the glowing flames of the flowers and the high, dark walls of Hampton Court.

Finally they went into the palace. They strolled through the lovely rooms admiring the fine pictures, splendid mirrors and delicately embroidered chairs.

Heather revelled in the needlework on the curtains of the ancient, four-poster beds.

They came out in the Tudor courtyard. Here they studied a wonderful old clock which told the days of the week, the seasons of the year and also had the signs of the zodiac painted on its blue face.

'I've just remembered something,' said Ronnie.

'And that is?'

'There is going to be a season of "Son et Lumiere" here in Hampton Court. So our next date at this place will be nine p.m. one evening.'

They had tea in the open-air restaurant. Then Ronnie put Heather on her train because that evening he had to put in an appearance at his club.

CHAPTER TEN

Dr. Martin West, F.R.C.S., studied the lovely, dark-haired girl as she opened and closed the door of his consulting-room behind her.

She replied to his greeting and then said:

'As the certificate for sick-leave absence, which I was given by a Margate doctor, has expired, I understand that I must come to you for a further certificate.'

'Sit down please. Just a minute.'

The doctor opened a drawer and took out some papers. He then studied Heather's dossier which had been forwarded from Margate.

He turned to Heather and smiled.

'How's the arm?'

'I feel on top of the world now that I've got rid of the plaster-cast.'

'Good! Now let me examine your right arm.'

After the examination he instructed her:

'Lift your hand above your head.'

She found that she was unable to do so.

The doctor made no comment but he

started to write.

After a minute he held out a paper and an envelope.

She saw that the first was a medical certificate.

Dr. West pointed to the address on the second envelope, saying:

'I want you to take this letter to the Physiotherapy Department of the Yeates Hospital. Do you know it?'

'I do, Doctor, and I started having physiotherapy treatment at The Emsham Hospital, Margate.'

'Yes, you really should have come to me as soon as you got to London. Then I would have arranged at once for you to have treatment.'

The grave expression on her face made him add in a reassuring tone, 'As your arm is a bit stiff the treatment will strengthen it and help to take away your stiffness and any possible pain.'

'May I go back to the school of ballet when this certificate has expired?'

Dr. West did not answer for a minute. From the girl's case-book and his examination as a surgeon, he doubted if she would ever be fit enough to dance or even teach in a school of ballet again. Now he had to decide to tell her the whole or only part of the truth.

He chose the latter course.

'"Limbering-up" in a school of ballet is very strenuous work, as equally strenuous as dancing in a *corps de ballet*. As you must realise, you've had a very nasty accident – a badly fractured arm, and cuts and bruises to your leg. Accordingly, for the present you must not teach in a ballet school – meantime get yourself a sedentary job.'

'But I love teaching ballet!'

'Sorry, but teaching dancing is quite out of the question at present. Besides, as I have furnished you with a medical certificate you will get sick pay. As the weather is so good, if I were you, I'd get out in the sunshine as much as possible. Now! Get off to the hospital and come and see me in a week's time.'

When his patient had gone Dr. West again studied the dossier sent in by the Margate hospital authorities. He noticed that the surgeon at The Emsham shared his opinion that it was unlikely that Heather Dean would ever dance again. Dr. West knew that, later on, he would have to decide the best time to tell the girl, not only that her career as a ballerina was finished, but also to mention to her that she must never again teach in a school of ballet.

From the expression that he had seen on his patient's face the doctor realised that she was upset that he had forbidden her to return to the Eglantine Ballet School the following week.

Dr. West could not blame the Margate surgeon, Mr. Smith, for deciding not to reveal to Heather Dean the fact that she would never dance again, but the doctor dreaded having to tell the girl the truth at some future date. She was a nice girl and he hoped she would get a good and pleasant sedentary job.

Heather walked away from Dr. West's surgery feeling rather despondent. She had counted on being able to write to Madame Eglantine to tell Madame that she, Heather, was returning in a week's time.

She thought, 'Thank goodness I'm meeting Ronnie tonight. He always cheers me up.'

When Heather reached the Yeates Hospital she walked along the front. On the right-hand side, adjoining the hospital, was a separate building. The girl guessed that it once had been a large house that had been taken over by the hospital authorities.

There was a board outside the building that carried the words:

PHYSIOTHERAPY
TREATMENT CENTRE

Heather went in the door that had *Entrance* on it.

She found herself inside a small hall in which several people sat waiting.

As she stood by the door one of the male patients said:

'If you're new go through that door.'

He pointed as he spoke.

Heather followed the man's instructions and found herself outside two small rooms both glass-fronted.

A woman in a white dress and white shoes came out of the nearest room.

Heather gave the nurse Dr. West's letter.

'I'll take this note in to Doctor straight away.'

She returned in a short time and ushered Heather Dean into the farthermost room.

The doctor asked the girl to sit down.

'I want to examine your injured arm,' he said. 'Please take off your sling.'

Heather did so.

After the doctor had examined her arm he

asked her to do certain movements with her right hand and arm.

'Bit stiff, aren't you?' said the medical man. 'I'll put you on a month's course here.'

He turned to the woman in white.

'Take the patient next door and instruct her when to come here,' he said. 'She can have her first treatment now.'

A few minutes later Heather discovered that the first thing she had to do was to put her arm on a pillow. Nurse then turned on a large lamp which was a fair height from the bed.

The nurse left Heather alone in the cubicle while the girl was having the lamp-ray treatment for her arm.

On returning the nurse asked the patient to do several exercises. In conclusion the elder woman said:

'Practise these exercises at home. Remember you can do *anything* now with your arm. Come along to the next room here I will put you on an apparatus to strengthen your right arm and help you to learn to raise it high above your head. We call it "The Pulley".'

Heather found herself in a long room which made her think of a gymnasium because at one end were parallel bars. She looked around her. At the other end two girls lay on beds evidently having sun-lamp treatment for their legs. Two older women were sitting with their feet in pails of healing liquid.

The voice of her nurse compelled Heather Dean's attention.

'You will take over from this gentleman. He will tell you what to do.'

So saying the attendant left the room.

Heather looked at the man nurse had indicated – he was sitting on a chair. Both his hands were grasping wooden rings attached to ropes fastened high up on the parallel bars.

He was in his twenties and would have been good-looking if it had not been for his pallor and the look of strain in his eyes.

Heather smiled. 'How well you can do it,' she remarked. 'I won't be able to lift both hands equally high as you do.'

'You will do so in time. Don't go too quickly and don't strain yourself, and stop and rest when you feel tired. Don't worry if you feel a sense of strain to your injured arm when you get home.'

'Were you badly injured?'

'I was paralysed,' he replied, 'and I hope to get all right. You see, I have a wife and child to keep. Now take over from me.' He watched her for a minute and said:

'Yes, you've got the hang of it, but don't forget to stop when you feel tired.'

He went over to an empty part of the room and taking a ball started bouncing it up and down.

Later her own attendant came in, adjusted the ropes and repeated what the man had said about not going too quickly.

A young nurse entered, smiled at the young man and started playing ball with him.

After a while the nurse said to the young fellow, 'You've got on quite well. Enough for the day, now get off home.' As she said this she put the ball away and went out of the room.

He picked up his coat, and going over to a mirror, smoothed his hair down. On his way back from the long glass the two women soaking their feet smiled at him. Later on, one of the women on the bed said something and laughed. He laughed back and coming over to Heather said:

'Good luck! And don't worry if you feel stiff when you get home.'

'I won't, and I think that *you* are doing splendidly.' Heather felt that she must say something encouraging to this patient.

A minute later the attendant came to Heather and said:

'Quite good! Stop now and come here the day after tomorrow. Is nine o'clock too early?'

'No.'

'All right! Here's your card, bring it every time with you. As soon as you arrive of a day place your card on this table. That will show me you're here. Good morning.'

'Good morning, nurse.'

As Heather was walking back to her flat her thoughts turned to the young man who had had paralysis. Tears came into her eyes as she thought of the way he had said so naturally:

'I *have* to get better. You see, I have a wife and child to keep.'

A little later, when she made for her rendezvous with Ronnie, she again thought of the man patient. Her mind also dwelt on the fact that she was not to be allowed back to the Eglantine Ballet School the following week.

So she was in rather a despondent and disappointed mood when she met the man she loved.

CHAPTER ELEVEN

The moment Ronnie saw Heather coming towards him he noticed the change in her. She was walking slowly. There was a listless and a dejected air about her that made the watching man feel that there was something wrong.

He jumped out of the car and greeted her, saying, 'Where shall we go today; would you like a long ride?'

Heather shook her head.

'Please, take me somewhere fairly near, because I have a lot to say to you.'

'Of course! Anywhere you like, dear.'

He studied her intently.

Yes, his first impression had been right. The joy of life seemed to have gone out of her face.

All at once he jumped to the reason for the change in the girl he loved. He remembered that this was the morning for her visit to the doctor. He said to himself: The doctor has probably told Heather that she must not return to her job in the school of ballet. It is

116

improbable that he has told her yet that she won't dance again, but whatever he *has* disclosed has made her look worried and depressed.

Aloud he said, 'As you don't want to go far, I'll run you along to some riverside gardens. They are just near Kingston-on-Thames where we went the other day. We can drink our tea sitting in deck-chairs and by the water's edge.'

'It sounds nice.'

'All right, dear. Let's go!'

After Ronnie had parked the car they walked through the gardens till they reached the refreshment chalet. Here he put Heather in charge of two deck-chairs while he fetched their tea from the little café.

After a while he remarked, 'You said that you had something to tell me. Is there anything wrong?'

'Well, yes! I went to Dr. West this morning.'

'What did he say?'

'That I was getting on nicely; but, on account of the injury to my right arm, that I must not go back to ballet yet, even to return to my job as a teacher of ballet. The moment I left the doctor, I wrote to Madame Eglantine telling her what the doctor said. I added

117

that perhaps she had better engage a permanent teacher in my place.'

'I think you are most wise to follow your doctor's advice.'

He leant over and patted her hand. 'Cheer up, dear, you must remember what a short time it is since you had that rotten accident. I mean, you can't expect to be perfectly well in a week or so.'

'Maybe, but I can't help feeling worried.'

'About what?'

'Well, *finance*. I mean, now I'll have to look for a clerical job, and I can't even type!'

'You poor sweet! Would you like a job in my night club?'

'Ronnie!' The old happy look came back again into her eyes.

He laughed as he answered. 'I see you *would!* Well, I'll get cracking about it at once.'

Heather smiled, but she pointed out, 'It's very good of you, dear, but what *could* I do in your cabaret? I mean, I can't sing and my doctor won't let me dance.'

He thought for a minute and then replied, 'I can offer you the role of a Fortune Teller. You will be billed as "Indira, the Lady Fortune Teller".'

'But I'm not an Indian, and I'm not a

fortune teller!'

'Nor was the last girl! Don't worry, my sweet! You'll be all right. In Indira's changing-room cupboard in my night club you will find all the former fortune teller's outfit – lovely embroidered saris, Indian costume jewellery, a make-up box, in fact "the lot". So you see you've nothing to worry about.'

'I'm not so sure of that! What about the fortune telling to start with? You see I know nothing about palmistry or fortune telling.'

'You haven't got to be an expert in these subjects. As I said a minute ago the act is a fake, but the members of a night club are persons who are out to enjoy themselves so they are not critical. Any charming and intelligent girl can take on this act. Later on, I'll tell you all about your turn.'

Ronnie's words had failed to banish the worried look from Heather's face. She said in a hesitant way, 'I know I'll be too scared to act in a cabaret.'

He laughed as he answered, 'Not *you!* Besides, you'll be assisted in the cast by a man who has experience of fake fortune telling and conjuring, Ali Chanderi used to do both turns at the entertainment at our Public School.'

Heather's face changed She started to

119

look interested. 'Tell me some more about my act.'

'Well, the curtain goes up and you are seen sitting on the floor. You are playing some notes on an Indian pipe. You haven't to be musical to do this. Ali Chanderi, the Indian conjurer, will teach you how to produce these few notes. As a matter of fact you blow into the pipe adjusting the stops as you do so – it is called a gourd pipe. The attendants will wheel on the stage a small cabinet. When this cabinet is opened twelve partitions are disclosed. In each of these partitions are a number of cards, on which are forecasted the fortune of a person born between certain dates – in other words born under a certain star. The cards also give the characteristics of a person born under such a star. Ali knows a bit about palmistry which he will teach you.

'Before you start your turn you make a little speech. You know the sort of thing! "Horoscopes for everyone – your characteristics – the best career – your life partner – lucky engagements, lucky dates and lucky colours – lucky date for a wedding – lucky dates on which to make an investment or a bet".'

Heather laughed and asked, 'What do I do after I have made my speech?'

'Invite members of the audience to come up on the stage to that you can tell their futures. Study your client intently then ask him or her the date of his or her birthday. Then pick out the appropriate card and tick on the card the characteristics which seem suitable. Read these out and also the person's fortune.'

'Do I do anything else in the programme?' Heather asked.

'Yes, you assist Ali Chanderi the magician of our outfit. Ali, as I think I said before, really is an Indian. He is one of the best fellows in the world and is a first-rate conjurer. Chanderi will like you because you are my friend. I've already told him about you and praised you to him. I've known Ali for years now. You see he was educated at the same public school as myself. He went to the Varsity about the same time as I sailed for Canada. Chanderi never finished at Oxford – he was "sent down" for a misdemeanour. He organised a Guy Fawkes rag. We kept in touch, and when my father died I wrote and told him that I was returning to England and asked him to come along and see me at the Delkushla. When he called he was full of trouble – his father, angered by Ali being sent down from Oxford, demanded that his son

121

came back to India. When Chanderi refused to do so Chanderi Senior cut off Ali's allowance. Remembering that Chanderi had been a first-rate conjurer at our public school I offered him the job in my cabaret. It was he who thought of and created the role of "Indira, the Fortune Teller".'

Ronnie paused and then said, rather anxiously, 'I *do* hope that you will find everyone very friendly in my night club. I think you will.' As he spoke he caught hold of her hand.

Heather gave Ronnie's hand a reassuring squeeze.

'Don't you worry! I'm going to be very happy – that is if I'm lucky enough for you to engage me.'

'Actually, *I* don't do any of the engaging – my manager, William Harcourt sees to all the matters relating to the staffing of the cabaret. But don't you worry, Heather. Harcourt, of course, will take you at my recommendation. Just come along to the club tomorrow and I'll fix it for you. The thing is, will you really accept the job?'

'I should say I *will*. It will be heaven being at the Delkushla.'

'No, far from that, but there is a friendly atmosphere at my club. The manager Bill Harcourt is one of the best, and the artistes are the nicest crowd you could ever meet.'

Heather resumed her questioning. 'Will I find the members of your Cabaret easy to get on with?'

'Yes, I think so, that is all but Carmen.'

'Carmen! Is she Spanish?'

'Yes, she was born in Madrid, but has become anglicised. Now she speaks perfect English. She is a personality dancer. Carmen does Spanish dances, Burmese dances, etc.'

'What does she look like?'

Ronnie knitted his brows. 'Well she would be rather a fine woman if she looked after herself. She drinks too much, and takes no exercise. Ali describes her as a lolloping, walloping...'

He broke off.

Heather smiled. 'You need not have stopped. You and Ali are not the only ones who have read about Swinburne's Roman Empress being a "lolloping, walloping trollop". By the way, is Carmen in love with you?'

'Oh! Making love to everyone she meets at the Delkushla is a habit of Carmen's. She is a "collector". My sweet, you're asking a lot of questions. By the way, now that we've finished tea, would you like to go on somewhere? I know a hotel near Burford Bridge where we could get an excellent high tea, or early dinner or what-have-you. Would you like to come?'

Heather jumped up. 'Yes thanks, Ronnie. Let's go!'

Later on, over an excellent dinner in the country hotel, the conversation again turned on the Delkushla.

'Tell me about the other people in your Cabaret,' said Heather.

Ronnie gave a short sketch of the principal artistes. He ended up by saying, 'As for the present, have you finished dinner, dear, or can I get you another cup of coffee?'

'No thanks, Ronnie. Everything has been perfect today. Thank you so much.'

'Well, my sweet, the day hasn't finished yet.'

'Meaning?'

'That this hotel has a beautiful garden and it's a lovely night, the moon is out.'

Heather laughed. 'And where is all this leading to?'

'A walk in the hotel's romantic-looking garden.'

He laughed and getting up collected Heather's bag and gloves and putting his arm through hers led her through the french window.

CHAPTER TWELVE

Next morning, Heather called at the Delkushla by appointment to see the manager, William Harcourt.

Heather put on one of her prettiest dresses and when Ronald Steele took her into Harcourt's office he felt proud of her. Before she called, Ronnie had sought out his manager and had told him about Heather Dean.

Harcourt, known at the night club as 'Daddy', studied Heather's pretty, vivacious face as he welcomed her, saying, 'Miss Dean, Mr. Steele has told me that you are thinking of joining us as "Indira, the second".'

'I haven't any experience of cabaret work.'

'In this particular turn experience doesn't really matter. Ali Chanderi is a very helpful fellow and he is most capable so I'm sure he will help you. Accordingly are you willing to have a shot at it?'

Heather smiled as she answered. 'Yes, please, Mr. Harcourt, and many thanks.'

'Well, I hope you'll be happy at the Delkushla. Now, as to salary,' here he mentioned the sum that was four pounds a week more than the sum Madame Eglantine had paid her.

Mr. Harcourt went on to say that the artistes at the Delkushla were given their food gratis. He then told her that she would find the saris, and everything required for her act, in the cupboard in the small dressing-room that was reserved for "Indira". He ended by saying that he would put her on the pay-roll at once.

'It's very good of you, Mr. Harcourt. Does that mean that I must go on tonight in the act?'

'No, my dear. I'll give you several days to get used to the club. Also, you will want to have rehearsals with Chanderi in private before you appear in public. No; for several days study Ali's act from the front. I expect you know that you are also to help him in his turn, hand him the props, etc. Ali is a good fellow and a great admirer of Mr. Steele, and he and, in fact, all of us will take care of you.'

Mr. Harcourt then turned to his employer and asked for his advice about another matter connected with the club. After that the manager hurried off on a pressing matter of business.

Half an hour later when she had met several other members of the Delkushla, Heather knew that she was going to be happy at the night club, because everyone had been so kind and friendly to her. Ali she liked at first sight. He was slim and handsome and spoke perfect English and had an Oxford accent. With a smile he explained the latter to Heather.

'Yes, Miss Dean, I was at Oxford and I had a fabulous time. I like to call myself a F.B.A. – Failed B.A.! Actually I was "sent down" for organising a rag on Guy Fawkes day which brought me into collision with the authorities. My old man stopped supplies. When I told Ronnie he offered me a job in his cabaret. Of course, I miss Dad's quarterly cheque.'

Heather's face expressed sympathy. 'Perhaps your father will come round,' she suggested.

'He *may!* But now to your affairs. I know quite a lot about conjuring work, so I shall be pleased to show you how the turn goes.'

The English girl smiled into the inscrutable oriental eyes and answered, 'You are very kind, no wonder Ronnie is always singing your praises. I do so hope I won't be awkward when I "feed" you in your turn.'

'You won't! But come along now and I'll rehearse you.'

Ali was very thorough. He went over the act several times till he was sure that she had got the hang of it. Finally he declared himself satisfied. He asked, 'Do you know how to put on a sari?'

'I don't.'

'Well, I shall get hold of Marie the singer to show you. Marie le Courteau used to help the first snake-charmer, I mean the original "Indira". Marie will show you how to dress for your act. There is an art in putting on a sari and also in the style of "make-up" if you wish to impersonate, successfully, an Indian girl. I'll direct you to Marie's dressing-room, and you ask her to show you how to dress. Then when you have got your sari on come back here and let me have a look at you. I'll give you a tip, get hold of one of the old saris and wear it about your flat or wear it about your room here, or, in fact, anywhere. If you wear your Indian clothes all day you'll get used to walking in them. Tomorrow night, if you like, you can help in my act.'

'Mr. Harcourt told me to see the show from the front tonight. He also said that I need not do my own act for some days.'

'That's right! Tomorrow I'll again rehearse you in your turn. We'll do it on the empty stage. I'll run over your act with you for several days. In this way you'll lose all fear of handling the snakes and will get perfect in your part.'

'Thanks, Ali, I'll go off now to Marie's dressing-room.'

'I'll take you to her door. Now, don't forget to show yourself to me when you have put on your sari.'

Heather liked Marie le Courteau at first sight. The Parisienne *chanteuse* was beautiful and vivacious. She had inherited golden hair from her English mother. She was bi-lingual. In addition to being very good-looking Marie had perfect 'dress sense'. In the cabaret she was billed as *'La Belle Marie – the* Parisienne *Chanteuse'*.

The two girls took to each other at sight. Marie followed Heather to the English girl's dressing-room. Here Marie taught her new friend how to put on a sari. Then Heather Dean returned to show herself to the Indian.

Heather found Ali most helpful. He showed her how to put the red caste mark between her eyes and how to darken the latter with kohl. He advised her to brilliantine her hair so as to produce the shininess of an Indian girl's coiffure.

Heather had just finished putting on her 'make-up' under Ali's guidance when there was a knock at the door. It was Ronnie.

'Miss Dean is here,' volunteered Ali. 'Marie has shown her how to put on a sari and I have taught her how to "make-up" so as to look like an Indian girl. Will you come in and give us your opinion?'

Ronnie was warm in his praise.

'You look like a dream from the Orient.'

'She's a houri!' exclaimed Ali.

'Yes – she'll be a good foil to our very scantily dressed dancers. Now, Heather! What about going now to your room and changing back into your English clothes? I'll give you half-an-hour to dress, then I'll come along and take you out to lunch.'

Ronnie turned to the young Indian and gave Ali the invitation:

'Would you like, also, to come along?'

Chanderi made a face. 'It's very good of you, but three is a rotten number. Thanks all the same.'

'Okay, Ali, have it your own way.'

A little later when Heather was facing Ronnie across a restaurant-table she felt that life was turning over a new page for her.

She determined to try and forget the last nightmare days of her stay in Nice – forget her broken career as a ballet dancer. Forget everything except her love for the man who was facing her – a man who was giving her this wonderful newly found happiness.

CHAPTER THIRTEEN

As the days went on Heather's life was a bitter-sweet one. From Marie and from other members of the cabaret she heard of Carmen's repeated efforts to get around Ronald Steele. Everyone told Heather that the Spaniard was very experienced sexually and would stop at nothing to involve her employer in an *affaire*. Consequently, sometimes Heather felt very happy, that was when she was alone with the man she loved. Sometimes she felt very miserable. It was a joy to Heather to see Ronnie every day, but it was a terrible worry to feel that Carmen was always on hand with her open, jealous antagonism and her pursuit of Ronnie. Over and over again the Spanish girl was to be found in Ronnie's room. If Heather ever collided with the Spaniard on such occasions and she remarked to Ronnie on Carmen's visits, he always vowed that the dancer had come in unexpectedly and against his orders and wishes. Heather believed him, but somehow Carmen's chasing of Ronnie rankled.

Marie le Courteau was the first one to warn Heather about the Spanish girl. The French *'chanteuse'* and Heather Dean had become fast friends. One day Marie said, 'You are fine in your act now, and already you are *very* popular in this night club. There is just one person you'll have to look out for.'

'Carmen?'

'Oh, I see you've heard about her. She's an alluringly nasty piece of work. Carmen Navada is a greedy, unprincipled woman. She's man-mad and has already taken two of the married men at the Delkushla away from their wives – one man is in the band, the other is a head-waiter – all fish go in Carmen's net. For months she even chased Ali, but he detests her, so she gave him up as a bad job. Now it is Ronnie Steele. Of course our young Head has everything – looks, money, and charm. Probably Carmen is planning to marry him, failing that if he stooped (which I'm sure he won't) she would be his mistress tomorrow. She's got a nasty, unhealthy passion for our good-looking employer and she'll do anything to get him.'

'And Ronnie?'

Marie threw back her head and laughed.

'Oh, Ronnie treats Carmen as a huge joke. That's what makes her so mad.'

'What did she do before she came here?'

'Acted as a so-called housekeeper to various men. The last man she lived with – to call it by its right name – was a scientist, quite a well-known man. He also made a name for himself as an expert in the matter of poisons. Fancy a scientist having anything to do with a girl like Carmen! She really hasn't one redeeming trait in her character. By the way, has she "warned you off the grass" yet?'

Heather protested. 'She wouldn't do that, Marie.'

'Oh, wouldn't she! You just wait and see.'

The days wore on; apart from worrying about Carmen, Heather's life at the Delkushla was a happy one. At first she felt extremely amateurish and nervous in her act, but Ali was invaluable in his help and support of her. She soon became friends with her audience. The other members of the club took Heather to their hearts and she soon became as popular as Carmen was unpopular with them. To start with any married woman in the cabaret or on the staff of the Delkushla knew that the Spaniard was perfectly unprincipled and capable of taking any of their husbands away from them.

One day Marie's warning to Heather (that Carmen would come to her room and tackle her about Ronnie) came true, because one Monday the door of Heather's dressing-room was thrown open and Carmen came in, smelling strongly of spirits.

The Spanish girl was drunk enough to be aggressive, but sober enough to know what she was saying and doing. She went straight to the point.

'Heather Dean, I want you to go away at once! I'll give you a week's salary, that will keep you till you get another job.'

Heather, who had been sewing, studied the tempestuous-looking girl who seemed to tower over her. When she spoke her voice was cool and disdainful. 'Perhaps you'll tell me why I should go away,' she said.

Carmen replied, 'Because you don't belong to the cabaret or the stage. I have heard how Ali taught you your job. You can't do anything.'

'That's a matter of opinion. Mr. Harcourt engaged me. My act is his business and he's satisfied with me.'

An angry flush came on Carmen's face.

She said venomously:

'You'll go away at once! If you don't something terrible will happen to you!'

Heather looked into the threatening, drunken face of the woman who stood before her. She asked in rather a sarcastic tone, 'And who says that some calamity will overtake me?'

'*I* do. I'll see that something awful happens to you if you don't go away. Before you came Ronnie Steele loved me and belonged to me.'

'That's a lie! An utter lie. Marie said that Mr. Steele would have nothing to do with you and just laughs at you.'

Carmen's face changed. She looked beside herself with rage. She exclaimed, 'Marie *dared* to say that! I'll settle with her! As for you, you little fool, you just look out! *I* can hurt anyone who stands in my path. So I give you one word of warning. Get out of the club.'

She flung herself out of the room slamming the door after her as she did so.

CHAPTER FOURTEEN

The following week Mr. Harcourt changed the order of the programme. Now Marie's act was to come early in the evening and was followed by Carmen's dance. Heather was not free till nearly the end of the performance. He also altered the opening to the fortune teller's act.

When her dances were finished Carmen looked around for an old lover of hers, Jerry Garland, who was still her willing slave. She found him lounging against one of the walls in the yard of the club. He had evidently popped out for a quick smoke.

Carmen went up to the young man, smiled into his eyes, and laid her hand persuasively on his arm, while she murmured in alluring tones, 'Jerry, darling, would you like to come round to my flat like you did in the old days?'

As she spoke she edged nearer him. Jerry could smell the heady, exotic scent which she used. Her hair brushed the young man's cheek that was nearest her.

He straightened up, and stretching his hands out to her he would have pressed her closer to him.

'No, Jerry! Not here! But I *will* arrange a "date" with you. I want you to do something for me.'

'Anything!' His voice had an eager note in it.

The Spanish girl smiled again and put her hand caressingly on his.

'All I want you to do is this – Ronnie Steele asked me to tell that precious new girl of his, Heather Dean, to come to his room immediately her act is finished and to say he wants her on important business. The snag is that she and I are not on speaking terms. As I don't want to go near her, will you?'

'Of course, Carmen, but you *will* let me in if I come around to your flat tonight, after the show is finished?'

'I'll let you in if that old hag of a landlady of mine isn't prowling around. A thousand thanks for promising to give Heather Ronnie's message.'

'Don't you worry. I'll go along at once and see to it.'

Carmen knew to a second when Heather was due to call at Ronnie's room. Two minutes previously, the Spanish girl had walked in unannounced. She smiled into her employer's eyes, saying:

'I'm afraid that I was catty in the things I said to you regarding Heather Dean but for your sake I'll be nice to her in the future.'

'I'm glad to hear you say it,' he answered. 'As you know, I *do* like a happy atmosphere in my club.'

Ronnie smiled and concluded, 'You're forgiven!'

Carmen said, 'Thank you so much.'

The Spanish girl could hear Heather's step outside. In a flash her arms were around Ronnie's neck and, drawing his mouth down to hers, she kissed him passionately. He was so astounded that he stayed still. They were like this when Heather, after giving a quick knock, walked in and found the couple in what looked like a close embrace.

Ronnie got away from Carmen. Then he turned around and faced the intruder.

When he saw that it was Heather he said, 'Blast!'

The English girl's head went up.

'Don't let me disturb you,' she said coldly.

'That's a childish remark!' flashed back Ronnie, who was furious at being found in such a position.

Carmen made for the door. She smiled an evil smile. On the threshold she said, 'Don't be late calling at my flat tonight.'

'Well of all the cheek and the lies! I'll be damned!' stormed Ronnie.

Heather's voice had a chilly note in it. 'I expect you'll say in a minute that you haven't promised to go around to Carmen's flat tonight.'

'Of course I'm not going to her place! I would never have dreamt of such a thing. I'm going to run you back to the door of your house, so hurry up and change.'

All at once Heather felt desperately tired. When she had come in the room and found Ronald and Carmen in what looked like a close embrace, she had received a shock. Now, all she craved was the relief from her troublesome thoughts and she felt that only sleep could bring relief to her tired mind.

Accordingly, she answered:

'I'll have to refuse your kind offer of a lift, because Marie is running me home. Good night!'

The door had shut behind Heather before Ronnie could say anything else to her.

And so the evening ended in a miserable way for Heather and Ronnie.

Next morning Ronnie determined to become reconciled with the girl he loved.

'I'll take Heather out to lunch,' he said to himself. 'When we are alone I can explain that Carmen came uninvited to my room last night.'

A little later, the owner of the night club left for the Delkushla because he knew that as it was a Sunday, Marie, Heather and several of the other girls came to the club to overlook their stage clothes.

Arriving at his night club, Ronald Steele made straight for Heather Dean's room.

After he had knocked three times and had received no answer, Ronald turned from the door. As he did so he almost collided with Marie.

'I'm looking for Heather,' he explained.

The French girl answered.

'Oh! Today she won't be coming along till half-past two. You see! Diane – you'll remember she's in your cabaret, well, it's Diane's birthday and she's asked Heather and some of the others to a luncheon celebration.'

Ronald's face fell. 'I *did* want to see Heather. In fact I came along to ask her to come out to lunch.' He paused and then said, reflectively, 'Of course, I could ask her to have dinner with me, but the trouble is that I really can't spare the time to stay here till half-past two.'

'You needn't wait here. Why not leave a note on Heather's dressing-table? Look!' – here Marie pushed open the door. 'Look!' she repeated. 'Heather's door isn't locked, you can go in there and write the note. When I see Heather I'll tell her your letter is on her table waiting for her.'

Ronnie's face lightened.

'Thanks for the idea, Marie,' he said. 'I'll write the note at once.'

Marie said good-bye and walked away while Ronald entered Heather's room and wrote a short letter to Heather asking her to have dinner with him that night at 6.30. He added the name of their rendezvous. He signed the letter, 'Yours, Ronnie.' Then he turned out his pocket in search of an envelope and not finding one left the note open on Heather's dressing-table.

Heather was very pleased to get Ronnie's invitation to dine that evening.

However, just before half-past six, as she approached the place which Ronnie had mentioned in his letter, she was surprised at his choice of a rendezvous. She knew that she had not made a mistake because she had memorised the address:

'The Elise, Henry Street, Soho.'

When she stood outside the building she saw that The Elise was not a restaurant but a café and a dingy, sordid-looking one at that.

The front door of The Elise was open and a bead curtain hung across the entrance.

Heather pushed her way through the hangings and when her eyes got accustomed to the half-light she saw that it was an ill-kept, foreign-looking room with a long bar at the far end.

There was a preponderance of men in The Elise.

Ronnie was not in the café. Feeling shy, Heather took a seat at a small, empty table near the door.

After she had been in The Elise for a little while Heather realised that the women present were of the lowest type. She said to herself, 'Why has Ronnie asked me to meet him in such an awful place?'

All at once the solution occurred to her – perhaps Ronnie wanted to interview some foreign artiste who had applied for a job in the cabaret of the Delkushla.

The air in the café was heavy with smoke. Heather had a sensitive throat, and she began to cough.

Several heads turned in her direction and she felt humiliated at attracting attention, and knew that only a drink would stop her cough.

She hesitated about going over to the bar because she felt that Ronnie might be annoyed if he saw her sitting drinking by herself.

A glance at the clock told her that Ronnie was now twenty minutes late and so really was not in a position to be critical. Also, her cough seemed to be getting worse.

So Heather crossed the room and sitting down on one of the high stools at the bar she ordered herself a drink.

The fat proprietaire grinned benevolently as he handed the glass to the young English girl.

Other men had started to look at Heather and when they caught her eye they grinned.

'Good evening!' Heather looked at the man who had addressed her. He was a continental and was huge, and ruddy-faced. The speaker was accompanied by a small, swarthy fellow. They had both sidled down the bar and now had taken seats at either

144

side of the girl and evidently were determined to get into conversation with her.

Heather's first impulse was to get up and walk out of the café, but the thought again occurred to her that Ronnie might be meeting a future 'turn' at The Elise – perhaps these two men formed a 'double act'.

One man spoke broken English to her. 'Are you American?'

'Oh, no. I'm English.'

Her answer seemed to amuse them.

'Would you care for another drink, chérie?' the man went on.

'Thank you, but I already have something.' Heather indicated the dregs of wine still left in her glass. At this they laughed and immediately got her another drink, and as she was afraid of giving offence, she accepted.

'*A vos beaux yeux,*' toasted the bigger man, clicking his glass with Heather's.

Then there was another drink with the proprietaire, and then there had to be more.

'No! Please, no more, thank you,' begged Heather, feeling her head reel under the influence of the strong, rough wine.

But the men only laughed thickly, pouring more of the liquid into her glass and pressing near to her; and as she felt their unpleasant breath against her neck and the contact of them against her, Heather was suddenly alarmed. She glanced quickly round. The proprietaire, as he polished glasses, smiled benevolently, firmly detached from the affairs of his clients. Then he vanished altogether. Through the smoke-hazy dimness, other, dark masculine faces grinned as they watched, while beside her, the two men were urging her with rough jocosity to accompany them to other cafés, for more drinks, etc.

'No, I must go home, let me go!' cried Heather in a sudden fright. Then one of the men, laughing as though he mocked her show of coyness, put an arm round her waist.

Panic now seized the girl and she struggled wildly – but suddenly the big brute was pulled away from behind and she staggered, almost falling against the counter. Trembling with fright, she turned and faced her rescuer, and found that it was the man she loved.

'Ronnie,' she stammered.

'It seems that I've come just in time!' he exclaimed.

He put his arm around her and then poured forth a flow of expostulation. Heather's would-be admirers, and in fact, the whole audience seemed to melt away from the fury of Ronald's white-hot rage. The proprietaire himself hurried forward from the back regions full of apologies and excuses, before any blame should fall on himself. Ronald Steele cut him short and, apart from a contemptuous gesture of dismissal, the young man paid no attention to anyone but Heather. Still frowning angrily he led her to the door.

When they got outside, Heather spoke to Ronnie again. 'Thank you!' she exclaimed. 'I don't know what I should have done if you hadn't come.'

'What a foul place!' Ronnie commented.

'Yes...' She added in a hesitant way, '*Why* did you ask me to meet you in such a café?'

'But I *didn't*, dear,' he replied. 'However we can't speak here. Let's cut through Soho Square to Oxford Street, and take a taxi to the hotel at which I asked you to dine, The Clifton, Marble Arch. When we reach our destination I'll tell you all about the "mix-up" this evening. Of course, dear, I'm deeply sorry that you've had such an unpleasant experience, but believe me when I say that it would have never entered my head to suggest that you even crossed the threshold of such a place as The Elise, the

147

character of which is visible at a glance, but I shall leave the telling of my story till we reach The Clifton.'

In a short while they were enjoying the perfect cuisine of the Oxford Street restaurant. At a pause between the courses Heather remarked:

'Did you really mean me to meet you here, at The Clifton? Your letter said The Elise, Henry Street, Soho, you know.'

Ronald shook his head. 'I never knew till about an hour ago that there even *was* such a place as the Café Elise. No, my rendezvous according to my note was here.'

A perplexed frown came on the girl's forehead.

'I am quite sure,' she replied, 'that the place you mentioned in your letter was the Café Elise.'

'That may be so, dear. Now look...' He took a paper from his pocket as he spoke, and he handed it to his companion. 'Look,' he repeated, 'the note I sent you has been tampered with.'

Heather studied the letter. 'I *did* notice,' she admitted, 'that you had erased some words and that you had printed 'The Elise, Henry Street, Soho' over the erased words, but I concluded that you had had second thoughts as to our meeting place.'

'No, dear, I *did* put "Clifton Hotel" in my message to you, and, in addition, I mentioned to Ali that The Clifton was the hotel in which we were going to dine.'

Heather put her hand to her head in a puzzled way. 'Sorry, Ron,' she replied, 'I just don't get you. To start with, how did you get your note back again, because I left it on my dressing-table at the club.'

'That's right. Ali Chanderi found the letter on the floor of your room. He picked it up – you know how tidy he is...'

Heather nodded in agreement.

'Well,' continued Ronald, 'as Ali put the paper back on to your table, he noticed the alteration which had been made in the letter. As he remembered my telling him that you and I were going to meet here, that is at The Clifton, his suspicions were aroused. Consequently Chanderi determined to meet me here at half-past six to warn me that something was wrong. When I got here tonight I found Ali waiting for me. He handed me your note and he told me what he suspected. As a matter of fact he thinks that Carmen came snooping into your room, and seeing the letter, she at once determined to send you to a place where she

149

hoped you would be insulted.'

'I see–' Heather examined the note again. 'Do you know,' she asked, 'if the words "The Elise, Henry Street, Soho" were written in Carmen's handwriting?'

'Goodness knows! I wouldn't like to say, but look! The words have been *printed* and you wouldn't have been suspicious of that because many people print *names*.'

'Yes, that's true.' Heather thought for a minute. 'I wonder,' she reflected, 'how Ali happened to be in my dressing-room?'

'Marie sent him in with one of your saris which she had taken away to iron for you.'

Heather nodded. 'I had forgotten that Marie said she would send my ironing back. Wasn't it providential that Ali *did* go into my room?'

'Yes, it was, dear. If he hadn't I might still be hanging about in this hotel lounge waiting for you. That, of course, wouldn't have mattered. The "bottom of the barrel" about this affair is that something grievous might have happened to you.'

Heather laughed as she answered.

'Let's forget about the whole affair.'

Ronnie nodded. 'How right you are. In the traditional words – "Let's eat, drink and make merry".'

The rest of the evening was a time of great happiness for Heather.

Later on Ronnie saw her to her door.

His last-night kiss was a long, lingering one.

CHAPTER FIFTEEN

Looking back on the next fortnight Ronnie knew that it was one of the happiest times for Heather and himself.

At the Delkushla, as they both avoided Carmen there was no discord. When Ronnie and the woman he loved were not at the club they spent as much time as possible together. Heather kept her nine o'clock appointment at the hospital.

As the spell of beautiful weather continued, every day while it lasted Ronnie called at Heather's flat in the morning. Then he drove her down into the country and they had lunch at some charming restaurant. When they had finished their meal they lolled in the sunshine. Later they would have an early tea and then Ronnie would get Heather back to the club in time for her to change into her Indian clothes.

As the good weather went on and on Ronnie and Heather continued their outings. They visited many of the beauty spots of Surrey – the old-world town of Godalming and the lovely spots of Dorking, Redhill, Brondbury or the rising land of Box Hill and the Epsom Downs.

All at once the good weather came to an end. So, also, did their happy and untroubled life. Ronnie knew that he would never forget the fête day at The Delkushla, because it coincided with the coming of Foster Jepson to the club, and the financier's appearance was the start of trouble for Heather.

Ronnie had been so moved by the appeal for help for the 'Save the Children' movement that he determined to put on a special programme one Saturday and to give all the money received at the club that evening to help the children in the eastern countries who were suffering from malnutrition. In between the cabaret shows at the club a collection was also to be made for the fund.

At the end of the rehearsal for the special cabaret show Ronnie had made a short speech to the members of his cabaret. He started:

'As you know, I do not encourage you girls to mingle with the guests and drink at the tables – with the exception of the dance-hostesses, of course. Tonight I am relaxing this rule because all the proceeds are to go to "Save the Children" fund. However, this does not mean that any of you girls are to put up with any liberties from any of the club patrons. If any of you have any trouble just appeal to Mr. Harcourt or myself. We shall both be in attendance all the time.'

Ronnie laughed. However, the girls knew by experience that their employer and his manager protected them and they knew that they got an excellent deal and worked under splendid conditions at the Delkushla, so they determined to do all they could to contribute to the success of the fête.

All the evening, or rather to the conclusion of the cabaret Heather had felt particularly happy. Her own item had been warmly applauded. Just before she had gone on the stage Ronnie had told her that she looked lovely.

At the conclusion of the cabaret all the performers reappeared together and received great applause.

Then the lights went up and the artistes, following Ronnie's instructions, left the stage and mingled with the audience. As the girl performers came into the main part of the hall many of the men present, especially if they were unaccompanied, jumped up, and invited the girl who was approaching, to have a glass of champagne with him.

Throughout the club there was the sound of laughter and an atmosphere of happiness.

Heather had left the stage. She felt shy so she hesitated as to what to do next.

A man at a nearby table rose and advanced towards her.

With a gasp of surprise and of horror she recognised the sardonic, evil-looking face of the man who had brought so much unhappiness to her in Nice, and had ruined her career in the *corps de ballet*.

He bowed as he reached her and said:

'Will the lovely lady entertainer drink to the success of the evening, in champagne, with me?'

Heather just stood there irresolute and utterly miserable.

Foster Jepson spoke again, this time in a whisper.

'People are looking at you, so it would be better to sit down and have a drink with me.'

As she went with him to his table and followed his instructions he whispered again.

'Smile, and try to look pleasant, otherwise people will think there is something wrong.'

He filled her glass with champagne and holding up his glass he toasted her, smiling as he did so. However, what he said to her was not very complimentary. He spoke in a low voice. 'Drink up and for the love of goodness say something!'

Heather took a draught of the champagne. It helped to steady her nerves. She answered Jepson, speaking in a low voice.

'Why *did* you come here?'

'To see you, of course!'

'But how did you know that I was at this club?'

'I called on Madame Eglantine and she told me about your accident and that you were now employed at the Delkushla Night Club.'

'Who gave you Madame Eglantine's address?'

'Your friend, Valerie Trent. I wrote to her, care of the *corps de ballet*, enclosing a stamped, addressed envelope.'

'Valerie was no friend of mine. Now, please go away at once!'

As he made no attempt to move, she said accusingly, 'Haven't you done me enough harm, as it is?' She repeated, 'Go away and don't you dare to come back! I never want to see your face again.'

'Ssh! Lower your voice and change the subject for heaven's sake. A tall, dark-haired man has been watching you intently. In fact, I believe he's heading for our table.'

Heather looked up and saw that it was Ronald Steele who was coming their way.

In an agitated but low tone of voice she said:

'It is my employer, the owner of the Delkushla who is making for our table.'

Ronnie looked concerned as he met the eyes of the girl he loved. Heather could feel that Ronnie sensed that there was something wrong with her.

However all he said was, 'And how is Indira, the talented fortune teller, getting on?'

'Quite all right, Mr. Steele,' she stammered.

But Foster Jepson had got to his feet and was pointing to the empty seat, saying:

'I shall be honoured if you will drink a toast to the success of your club fête with me?'

'Thanks!' Ronnie's words were directed to Foster Jepson, but his eyes had never left Heather's face.

Ronnie sat down. He smiled at Heather; it was a warm, loving smile.

Jepson poured out a glass of champagne and handed it to the club owner.

'Cheers.'

After Ronnie had said this he turned to the silent girl and enquired in solicitous tones:

'Is everything all right? Do you want my help?'

Heather's heart went out in love and gratitude to the kind, handsome man she loved so dearly. For the first time since she had sat down at the table she smiled as she answered.

'No, but thank you very much all the same.'

Meantime Foster Jepson had taken a cheque book and a fountain pen from his pocket and was now busily writing.

In a minute or so the financier tore a cheque out of his book and had handed it to the club owner saying, 'This is for your "Save the Children" fund.'

'£200,' Ronnie exclaimed. 'This is most generous of you, Mr.–' here Steele's eyes wandered to the cheque, 'Mr. Jepson.'

Ronnie looked around because at this minute there was a fanfare of trumpets and the Lovelies, accompanied by the club manager, appeared with collecting boxes.

Ronnie pointed to Mr. Harcourt who was approaching their table.

'Mr. Jepson,' said Ronnie, 'wouldn't you

like to give this generous cheque yourself to my manager? Here he is.'

Heather took advantage of Mr. Harcourt's appearance to say:

'Will you excuse me, Mr. Steele, but Marie has relatives here tonight, and I promised to meet them.'

Jepson rose. 'It's been a pleasure to renew our acquaintance, Heather – I'll have to come again soon to the Delkushla.'

She nodded farewell and turned away. Before she could reach the next table she felt a hand on her arm. It was Ronnie.

He questioned her in a low voice, 'Is anything wrong, dear?'

'No, why do you ask that?'

'I was going by your face. You look upset. Has that fellow been worrying you in any way?'

She was silent.

Ronnie went on, 'That man Jepson said that he had met you before. Is that true?'

She knew that she couldn't lie to the man who meant so much to her.

She replied in nervous tones, 'Yes, Ronnie, but would you be so kind as to excuse me now, because I really have an engagement with Marie.'

'All right, darling, but remember, if you

have any worries, well, just bring your troubles to your boss and let him make everything right for you!'

Heather's eyes registered love and affection as she replied in a low voice, 'I'll remember, Ronnie, and thank you very much, dear.'

She turned away and made for a table where Marie was entertaining several guests. Ronald's eyes followed Heather. He felt a fierce resentment against Foster Jepson because he was sure that the man had said something to worry Heather. Probably the very sight of the fellow had reawakened some unhappy memory. He wondered if Jepson had had anything to do with Heather's failure in the *corps de ballet*. Ronnie determined to protect Heather in every way from Foster Jepson and in so doing discover the unhappy secret of Heather Dean's past.

CHAPTER SIXTEEN

After the fête given by The Delkushla to help the 'Save the Children' fund Foster Jepson went frequently to the night club. His sole object in going there was to see Heather Dean. From the first day on which he met her he had been overwhelmed by a devastating passion to possess her, not only because she was a very lovely and a very attractive girl but because of her uncanny likeness to a girl in his past, Lorna Mannering. Jepson had tried to get Lorna by the power of his money. However she had scorned and eluded him. Now he had a mad passion for her counterpart, Heather Dean.

At the Delkushla, Foster Jepson tipped lavishly. He thought this might prove useful if he broke some of the club rules such as going behind the 'scenes' or wandering down the private corridor of the matchwood wall – the way that led to the rooms of the club officials and to some of the artistes' dressing-rooms. After a number of visits to the club he sensed that Ronald Steele greatly admired Heather and he felt that the girl was in love with her employer.

That night as he watched Heather's act his passion for the young girl was rekindled. He thought, she's got everything to attract a man.

A bitter hatred for Ronald Steele entered the financier's mind as he sat there listening to the applause from the audience at the end of Heather's act.

A plan entered Jepson's mind. From something he had witnessed the night before he felt that there was one person at the club who would help him to come between Heather Dean and her employer and that person was Carmen the Spanish personality dancer. Late that night the owner of the club had been having refreshments at a table and when the Spaniard had passed by she had laid her arm in an affectionate way on Ronald's arm. Steele had said something in a low voice. Jepson guessed it to be a snub because Carmen Navada had flushed and passed on. The incident had been slight, but it had shown Foster how the land lay.

At this particular moment the financier was having something to eat and drink at one of the upstairs tables. Ronnie passed through the private door and was shortly followed by Carmen.

The financier glanced around to see if anyone was watching him. When he was sure that he was unobserved he, too, went through the door of the matchwood partition. He was just in time to see Carmen opening the door, which previous experience had taught him, had the club owner's name on it.

Jepson crept stealthily to the door of Ronald Steele's room.

Noticing that it was not quite shut he gave it a gentle push which opened it sufficiently to let him hear what was going on in the room. Ronnie was saying in irritable tones:

'Carmen, you know I forbid artistes to come to my private room unless I send for them. Now clear out at once!'

'Oh, Ronnie dear!' the Spaniard exclaimed. 'Don't send me away. I love you.'

Jepson saw Carmen suddenly throw herself into Ronald's arms.

A light step coming down the corridor made Foster draw back and hide himself in an adjoining doorway. He peered round the corner and grinned in an evil way as he saw that the newcomer was Heather. He guessed that Ronald had sent for the young girl.

Now for a row! the financier thought.

Jepson proved right because in a few seconds Ronnie opened the door and put Carmen out of it.

With a flushed, frustrated face the dancer bounced away. Jepson followed the Spaniard to her room. He stood at the door and said:

'May I introduce myself? My name is Foster Jepson. I want to congratulate you on your wonderful dancing. I was wondering if you'd perform at a private performance for a charity I'm interested in? You would get a fee, of course.'

The dancer was evidently puzzled. At length she remarked:

'What are you doing around here at the back? It's not allowed, you know. If the manager, Mr. Harcourt sees you, you're for it!'

'I hardly think so. You see, I gave Mr. Harcourt £200 for the "Save the Children" fund. Now may I come in and discuss the fee that you'll get for dancing at that charity performance?'

'Oh!' Carmen was visibly impressed by the sum of money Jepson had given to the club charity. She felt that a man who could shower £200 cheques about was worth entertaining. She said effusively, 'Come inside.'

Jepson entered. She motioned to a chair. He lit her a cigarette and as he did so, lifted up the sleeve of the silk flowing housecoat that covered her scanty jewelled briefs. He murmured, 'Have you to cover up your beautiful self?'

Carmen laughed and going over to a cupboard brought out a bottle and two glasses.

'Have a drink?' she invited.

'If you'll let me pay for it.' He placed a note on the table.

A pleased look came into the dancer's eyes. She took the money, murmuring, 'As you will, and thanks.'

She poured out the drinks and then gave the toast 'Down the hatch!'

'No, here's to our further acquaintance,' he replied putting his arm out.

He whispered, 'My dear, you have a perfect figure and are a very lovely girl.'

She murmured sulkily, 'Some people don't think so.'

He pressed her hand and hazarded, 'You mean Ronald Steele?'

Carmen disengaged herself, and looking into his face, said in a surprised tone, 'How did you know?'

'I was passing and saw your exit from Mr. Steele's room.'

Jealous tears came into the girl's eyes. She said passionately, 'It's all the fault of that little cat Heather Dean. I'll not rest till I "hoof" her out of this club. I'll separate the two of them. I'll do anything in the world to prevent her marrying Ronnie Steele.'

'That suits me, too.'

The cold vindictive tones of the financier startled Carmen. She exclaimed, 'Hi! What are you driving at?'

Jepson took out his cheque book. 'I mean that if you make it impossible for Heather Dean and Ronnie Steele to marry I'll give you the same big cheque as I gave Mr. Harcourt.'

'Two hundred pounds?'

'Yes, two hundred pounds.'

Carmen sat up. 'Agreed! I'll do it by some means or other. But tell me–' a sly and puzzled look came into her eyes – 'I don't see how you come into the picture.'

Foster Jepson thought quickly and decided to lie. 'I come into the picture, my dear, because I want to be avenged on Heather Dean. She was my secretary and left me in the lurch, for she walked out on me at my busiest time. It was a dirty trick and I won't forget the way she let me down. She fancies herself, too – God knows why, because she's a plain-looking piece. She hasn't your face and wonderful figure.' His arms went around her and his voice sank to a whisper, 'I shall dream of you tonight. If you manage to separate Heather Dean and Ronald Steele, come along and tell me, and I shall see that you are rewarded.'

Carmen nodded. 'I'll come and before a week is out I'll earn that two hundred pounds.'

'Good girl! Here's my phone number. You let me know the moment you've done the deed, and within an hour the money will be yours.'

Carmen pressed his hand. 'You'll make it cash, won't you?'

'All right; and don't forget, if you come round for it yourself and *stay* – well, I'll make it a much larger sum.'

'Don't you worry! I'll come and I'll deliver the goods. But I think you ought to go now. Daddy Harcourt is a bit on the warpath these days. You see, these gossipy cats here have complained to him about me.'

'I know! Just because they are jealous of your good looks – afraid they will lose their men-folks to you, eh?'

'Something like that.'

Jepson rose. 'Well, Carmen, I don't want

Harcourt to have "a down" on you so I'll get off at once. But you *will* come and stay with me, won't you?' He kissed her passionately.

A step in the passage outside caused him to release her. He made for the door, saying, 'You won't forget our bargain, will you?'

'What do you think?' she laughed. 'I'll get that two hundred pounds somehow. You'll see!'

When Jepson laughed, a reflective look came into Carmen's eyes. She spoke her thoughts aloud– 'But – how?'

That night when she watched the second performance of Heather's act she got the answer to her question.

CHAPTER SEVENTEEN

Mr. Harcourt had called a morning rehearsal as he had engaged some new performers. He had also introduced some fresh business into the cabaret programme. When the rehearsal was over, as the performers were not required till the evening, they started to disperse.

Ronnie, who had been watching in the wings, stopped Heather and Marie as they were coming off the stage. They started chatting together. Ali joined them.

'That's your nicest sari,' said Marie.

Heather looked at herself in the glass. Her face and arms were stained to make her look like an Indian girl, but it was a light, attractive shade. She had on a sari of pale, lime-green with a border of heavy gold which served as a frame to her vivid face and dark hair. With the sari was worn an underjacket of gold brocade and the same material had been used for her bag and shoes.

Ali made his usual comment, 'She's a houri!'

Ronnie smiled and gave the invitation. 'Are you coming out to lunch, Heather?'

'I'd love to, but I shall have to spend the rest of the morning sewing. Half this border is loose' – she pointed as she spoke, 'and if I don't look out it will come off and trip me. It is very good of you to ask me out, but I feel I must see to my sari, so I'll get something to eat here in the club.'

'I quite understand.' Steele turned to the Indian, 'Are you coming?'

Ali nodded so Heather waved farewell to Ronnie, saying, 'See you tonight!'

Marie stayed behind for a few minutes talking to Heather. Then she left for her flat.

When the French girl had gone Heather went into her room, changed and started sewing the border on to her green sari.

All at once there was a knock at the door. She called, 'Come in!'

An attendant entered, saying, 'A gentleman to see you, Miss Dean.'

Heather jumped up in her surprise because she found that she was facing Foster Jepson the man who had treated her so badly at Nice and ruined her career.

When the commissionaire had gone Jepson shut the door and made for a chair, saying, 'May I?'

Before he sat down he pushed the other easy chair towards her. Almost unconsciously she sank into it.

Foster Jepson smiled and handed her an envelope.

'What's this?' she asked.

'Well, when we met on the Continent, you complained that you had been robbed.' He opened the envelope and pushed a cheque towards her. 'This,' he went on, 'is just a little present of money to make up for your loss.'

As Heather sat motionless and made no attempt to take the money Jepson went on:

'Take the cheque! I'm a rich man. I get plenty of money.'

She looked straight into his eyes. 'I wonder how you *do* get your money. My sixth sense tells me that you earn it dishonestly. I also think that you collaborated with the manageress of the café in Nice in goodness knows what dirty business. Through you, I lost my chance in the *corps de ballet.*'

'Well, now I want to help you. Leave this club and come and stay with me. I shall give you everything that a woman loves – money, jewels, furs and elegant clothes. You are very beautiful. I think that a beautiful woman should have a beautiful setting. You're out of

171

place here with these mountebanks.'

Heather looked very annoyed. She said indignantly, 'The performers are clever, hard-working people. They've got decent characters. Everyone has been very kind to me.'

'That may be true, but it doesn't alter the fact that you're like a fish out of water here. Come away with me now.'

He jumped up and catching hold of Heather's hand pulled her to her feet.

'If you come to me I shall see that you will never have to do a stroke of work again. All the beautiful things that you must have longed for all your life – will be yours.'

She got away from his encircling arms, and going to the door threw it open. She demanded:

'Are you going? Or shall I have you thrown out?'

'I'll go if you will come with me.'

As he again made a move towards her she said, 'Now listen, Foster Jepson, as you won't move out of my room, I shall go away for a few minutes and if you are still here when I come back I'll call for help from the attendants. This place is never quite empty so if you remain I'll call on the commission-aires to throw you out. And another thing!

Don't you dare to come back on any future occasion.'

She walked out after she had said this.

Jepson stood by the open door. A tall attendant came down the passage. He said to the financier:

'Is there anything I can do for you, sir?'

The man's voice was pleasant and respectful, but he stood his ground. Without answering the young commissionaire, Jepson picked up his hat and went out of the club.

That night as Foster Jepson lay awake his mind turned on Heather Dean. An image of her beauty came before him. He knew that it was her elusive quality as well as her physical beauty which attracted him.

Foster Jepson realised that all his life he had had two cravings – love of money and love of women. Since he had gained a fortune he had not had much trouble in gratifying his second desire.

His face darkened as he recalled Heather's remark that morning. 'My sixth sense tells me that you get your money with dishonesty. I think you collaborated with the manageress of the café in goodness knows what dirty business.' Of course it was only a shot in the dark as far as Heather Dean was concerned, but he realised that Heather was one of the girls he could not buy.

As he thought on in this way he suddenly remembered a girl he had known twenty years ago, the girl whom Heather Dean greatly resembled. Heather, like Lorna, had been unattainable. Like Heather Dean, Lorna Mannering had been dark-haired. They had the same coloured eyes and were of similar build.

Lorna had been practically penniless when she had come to his office seeking employment. Attracted by her beauty he had at once given her the clerical vacancy. In an embarrassed and hesitant way she had asked if she could have some of her weekly wage in advance, because she had no money at all and she wanted the cash for board and lodging.

Jepson had studied the girl, Lorna Mannering, as she stood before him. He could tell that she was nervy and run-down. In spite of this the girl was beautiful. She had magnificent black hair, great dark eyes, vividly red lips and she carried herself gracefully.

He had paid Lorna Mannering's wages in advance and she had been grateful. Later on he had made unmistakable advances to the brunette – advances which she had instantly repulsed. When he had renewed his proposal she had walked out on him. He would never forget the contempt in her face and the scorn in her voice as she made for the door.

He had kept track of Lorna when she left him and discovered that she had got herself another job.

After a short time he renewed his attentions. Lorna ignored his letters and his messages. As soon as she knew it was his voice on the phone she put the receiver back. When he finally forced himself on the girl, she told him plainly, and in no uncertain terms, how utterly abhorrent he was to her.

Jepson had taken a long time to get over the wound inflicted by the dark and penniless beauty. Now he knew that Lorna Mannering had been reincarnated in the personality of Heather Dean. The two girls could have passed as twin sisters.

The financier lay there vainly trying to get off to sleep. Till tonight he had thought seldom about Lorna Mannering. Probably it was Lorna's strong likeness to Heather Dean that had recalled her to memory. In an angry, irritated way he had remembered

Lorna's refusal of him and this made him all the more determined to try again to get Heather for himself. He could not marry the young girl because his wife would not divorce him. He would do his uttermost to get Heather and if he failed to do so he'd move heaven and earth to prevent Ronald Steele marrying Heather.

As he lay there planning the future a wave of unbalanced thoughts took possession of the financier.

He said to himself, 'As Carmen has promised to separate Heather and Ronald Steele and so prevent them marrying one another, for some days I'll leave things to the Spanish girl and so I won't go to the Delkushla till I get in touch with Carmen again. If the latter fails me, I shall again seek out Heather and I'll offer her a very large monthly settlement if she comes to live with me. If Ronnie Steele gets in the way of my wishes I'll dispose of him somehow.'

If anyone had been in the financier's room at that moment, and had been able to study Jepson's face, the onlooker would have thought that he was looking at the face of a madman.

If any of Foster Jepson's city associates had been told of the way he had criminally made money on the Continent and had now been told of what he was planning to do to Ronald Steele, such business colleagues of Jepson's would have thought that their sober-looking millionaire friend had gone suddenly mad. A specialist would probably have attributed Foster Jepson's mental state to schizophrenia.

Jepson took a cigarette from his bedside table, lit it and returned to his original train of ideas. He consoled himself with 'If the worst comes to the worst, I feel I can look to Carmen for help. That woman is money-mad and I know she is determined to earn that two hundred pounds that I've promised her.'

Letting his thoughts run in this vein, Jepson at length fell off to sleep.

CHAPTER EIGHTEEN

There was a thoughtful look on Carmen's face as she watched Heather's act that evening. The young English girl had entered to applause, for the audience had remembered her from the previous turn in which she had helped Ali. Also, they liked her appearance. Tonight she was in a brilliant crimson silk sari, which had a heavy gold border. There was a scarlet flower in her black hair. Her bag and shoes were of red and gold brocade.

Heather salaamed to the audience, and seated herself, Indian fashion, on a pile of cushions on the floor. Ali followed her, accompanied by an attendant who pushed in the small cabinet which held the horoscope cards.

At the conclusion of Heather's fortune-telling, Ali reappeared and he and Heather collaborated in the finale of their double turn. This took the form of a disappearing trick. Ali forces Heather to get into a large box, and a secret lift running down to the basement, Ali makes Heather disappear. He shows the audience the empty box.

When Heather appears from the back of the audience, Ali does his final trick!

Pretending to wish to show his appreciation of Heather, he pours her out a drink from his magic kettle. However, as it is only water, the girl rejects the drink. Thereupon Ali presses a secret spring and wine pours from the kettle, into Heather's glass.

During the part of the performance when Heather was pretending to be afraid – a memory of a great fear came back to Carmen – the memory of how *she*, too, had been frightened to death at the thought of the poisons possessed by the owner of the house when she had been living with Christopher Banks, the scientist. 'Deadly instantaneous poisons'. She repeated the words to herself. Poison! How she wished that it was a deadly poison that Heather was drinking now, for then her rival would die and leave the road clear for her, Carmen, then she could marry Ronnie.

The Spanish girl looked at the stage again, and a hot, jealous feeling came into her heart, for Ronnie was standing in one of the wings at the other side of the stage. 'He's watching her as if she were precious as gold,'

Carmen said angrily to herself.

As she looked at the scene on the stage the dancer's thoughts went back to her former lover, Christopher Banks. She had gone with him one day to a store in the East End of London, where he had purchased, among other things, a bottle of cyanide. The description of the poison had attracted Carmen–' 'Cyanide usually causes instantaneous death'. So when the opportunity arose the Spaniard stole a small quantity of cyanide.

A bitter look came into Carmen's eyes as she thought of her last day with the scientist. How cruel Christopher had been as he practically threw her into the street. He had no heart. She hated him, for he was cold and cynical. He had turned her out of the house without a penny. Christopher Banks had returned unexpectedly in the early hours of the morning from a trip to the north of England, and he had caught her with a lover. The man had fled, leaving her to face Christopher alone. He had only smiled sardonically, however, as he put her out of the front door, saying, 'Good luck to you with your new lover, and your new *profession!*' He had been cold and heartless. Ronnie was not like that. He was young, warm and handsome. If only Heather could be got rid of! If Heather were only out of the way!

By next evening, Carmen had made up her mind to kill Heather Dean, and had determined to do so during the evening performance. She had brought from her flat the small bottle of cyanide poison that she had stolen from Christopher Banks.

When Carmen reached the club, she saw to her relief that it wanted nearly two hours to the evening performance.

She knew that Heather would not be there for another hour. Before she let herself into the English girl's room, she looked around and saw to her relief that there was no one about. Once inside the room, she shut the door and hurried over to the table where Ali had left his 'magic kettle', and some others of his smaller 'props'. These, Heather took charge of, and brought them down to the stage just before Chanderi's act. Carmen knew that the 'magic kettle' contained a secret compartment holding wine. Ali poured out this wine by releasing a magic spring.

Carmen took the lid off the magic kettle, then, by touching a spring, she opened the secret compartment holding the wine. Next she took the bottle containing the cyanide from her bag, and poured some of the poison into the wine. She shut the secret compartment, and replaced the lid of the kettle. Then she made for the door. When outside, she almost collided with a man who was passing. She saw to her annoyance that it was the Indian conjurer.

'Hello, Ali,' she stammered.

He looked searchingly at her. His quick eyes took in the case under her arm. He glanced towards the door out of which she had come, and a puzzled expression came on his face, and he asked himself, 'Why has that woman been to Heather's room?'

Aloud he said, 'Good evening, Carmen,' but the Spanish girl was almost out of hearing as he spoke.

He thought for a little while, and then, unable to answer his own question, made for the bar.

CHAPTER NINETEEN

As Ali prepared for his conjuring act his thoughts kept running on Carmen. Why had she looked so confused when he had caught her coming out of Heather's room? Guilt had been written all over her face. What had she been doing in Heather's room at all? Everyone in the Delkushla club knew that the two women were bitter enemies.

He paused in the act of putting his 'props' ready to hand and again he tried to solve the mystery. After a little while he gave it up, but determined to watch. He made up his mind not to worry Heather by telling her about Carmen's visit to her room, but he might warn her to be careful.

Immediately before the conjuring act he said to her, 'Do you lock your dressing-room door when you're out?'

'No, Ali. Why?'

'Most people do, Heather. It's wiser to do so. If not, you may have things stolen.'

'But I don't bring anything of value to the club.'

'For all that, I would lock my door, if I were you.'

The beginning of their act prevented further conversation. They received an ovation. Ali's brilliant conjuring, enhanced by Heather's beauty and charm, made the audience applaud loudly.

When the Indian turn was over, three other items followed; then it was time for Heather to appear in her Fortune-Teller's act. Ali's work in this turn was slight. He took no part in the actual fortune telling. This was followed by a vanishing act.

In conclusion he uses his magic kettle to offer Heather a drink – first a glass of water which she rejected, then some wine which she drank.

At the opening of the act, when the band was quietly playing a short introduction of appropriate Oriental music, Ali noticed that someone had come in and was watching the act intently. He looked across and saw that it was Carmen, but her eyes were not on Heather or himself; they were riveted on the magic kettle which was on a table. On her face was a strange expression – a combination of malevolent triumph and hatred. Again Ali recalled Carmen's visit to the English girl's room.

Time passed! They had completed the vanishing act, and were at the finale where Ali offers Heather first a drink of water, and then a drink of wine.

As Heather rejected the glass of water, Ali looked across to where Carmen was standing. Now the Spanish girl had a look of ferocious malevolent triumph on her face. This puzzled the Indian, but as he poured out the glass of wine which was quickly taken out of his hand by Heather *he knew!* Because from the wine came the singular smell, characteristic of one of the most deadly of poisons. Ali was back in memory, in the science lab of his Public School, he recalled his science master saying, 'Cyanide is an immediate and nearly always, a fatal poison. It has a singular and arresting odour as you will now notice as you smell it.'

Ali now realised that Carmen, in her attempt to poison Heather, had put cyanide in the wine. The Indian's face was convulsed with fear. The audience, taking his performance as all part of the act, applauded vigorously.

With a quick movement Ali knocked the glass out of Heather's hand. It broke into pieces, spilling its contents as it fell. The Indian could see that Heather was greatly

185

surprised and rather upset, but the audience applauded again, and so the girl went on with the rest of the turn, bowing to the audience and kissing her hand to the men and women who were present.

The item finished to great and sustained clapping.

Heather went straight to her dressing-room, and, as Ali was following in her wake he felt a tap on his arm. It was Ronnie, who greeted him with, 'I won't keep you a second, Chanderi, but I was watching your face when you smashed that glass. There was something wrong? What was the matter?'

The Indian hesitated for a second, and then answered, 'I'll tell you everything if you promise not to repeat it to Heather. I don't want her scared and worried.'

Ronnie looked into the dark, earnest face in front of him. He knew how sincere the Indian was, so he answered, 'All right, Ali, I swear I won't tell anyone.'

'Well the wine that Heather was going to drink tonight had cyanide in it. If I had not smashed the glass and spilt the contents, Heather would be dead by now!'

Ronnie grew deadly pale, and exclaimed, 'Good God!' Then, after a pause, he questioned, 'But who on earth could have put the poison in the wine?'

Ali's face took on a stern expression. 'Carmen! I banged into her as she was coming out of Heather's room this afternoon. She got awfully red and confused when she saw me.'

Ronnie wrung his friend by the hand. 'What can I do for you in return for saving Heather's life?' he said.

Ali grinned, saying, 'Oh, it was nothing. You've both been so decent to me.'

Ronnie passed his hand over his forehead. He looked as if he were about to faint.

Chanderi turned to go, explaining, 'It's getting late. I'll push off.'

'But what about Carmen?'

Ali said earnestly, 'Leave her to me. We Indians have our way with murderesses.'

Ronnie looked at the Oriental's poker face. It told him nothing, but he knew he could rely on his friend not to do any violence, so he answered:

'All right, and thanks a lot. I wish to heaven we could "hoof" Carmen out of the club!'

'We *shall!* I'll force her to leave the club tonight!'

Ronnie took Ali's hand and wrung it warmly, saying, 'Thanks again, Ali. You were great – a good show!'

The Indian finished his cigarette, then he made for Carmen's room. He entered without knocking.

The Spanish girl had not yet changed her dress. She was sitting, moodily smoking. She looked up at his entrance, and an expression of fear came into her face.

Ali greeted her with the one word – 'Murderess!'

'Get out, you Indian swine!' She almost spat the words at him.

Ali went over and took her roughly by the shoulders. 'Murderess! But, luckily, your criminal plans miscarried. Nevertheless, you planned to kill Heather by putting poison in her drink!'

'It's a lie,' she cried, but her face blanched.

'It's not, and you know it.'

'You can't prove it.'

'Oh, yes, we can. You didn't realise that you left *your* finger marks on the secret compartment in the kettle that held the wine. So if you don't want to be arrested, you'd better clear out of the club at once.'

Carmen's lips set in a stubborn line. 'I'm not going!' she exclaimed.

The Indian shrugged his shoulders. 'That will be *your* funeral. Perhaps you don't know the term of imprisonment you will get for an attempted murder? Believe me, the sentence won't be a light one.'

Carmen suddenly appeared to break down. She dissolved into loud sobs, but the man saw that there was not a tear in her eyes.

After a while he said roughly, 'Shut your trap and clear out! As you only use this room to dress in, you can't have much to pack. I'll give you ten minutes to go. Now get busy!'

The woman studied the Indian's relentless face. She knew she had met her match. Five minutes later she was dressed ready to go. When she got to the door, she said with assumed pitifulness:

'You're a brute to throw me out like this, for I'm penniless and friendless! I shall starve!'

As he watched her out of the front door of the club, Ali commented, 'She *won't*. Her sort never starve.'

Ronnie was so upset by Ali's revelation regarding Carmen's plot to kill Heather that he felt that he must see her before she left the club. He knew that his time alone with her would be of short duration, because, soon after she had changed out of her Indian costume, she would be leaving in Marie's car for her flat in Norbury.

So, after giving Heather sufficient time to change, he knocked at the door of her dressing-room.

Heather looked surprised to see him. She laughed and said, 'I thought you were Marie.'

'Oh, yes, she generally drops you on her way home, doesn't she? May I come in?'

'Of course, Ronnie!'

She motioned to a chair, saying, 'Won't you sit down?'

Although he said 'Thanks,' he remained standing.

Heather didn't speak, because she sensed that something had upset Ronald. She waited.

He caught hold of both of her hands. 'Are you all right, darling?' There was an urgent note in his voice.

'Why, yes, dear. Do I look ill?'

'No, but at the end of your act you *did* look a bit upset.'

Heather laughed. 'Oh! I remember now! I don't know if you were watching my act, but Ali went mad and dashed my glass to the ground before I drank the wine.'

'Yes, I saw it, and didn't the audience

applaud you and Chanderi.'

She nodded. 'I never remember getting such an ovation, but I must say that Ali acted so realistically that he startled me.'

'Poor old darling!'

All at once a great wave of love and desire took possession of Ronnie. The thought that he had nearly lost her by death made him determine to tell Heather that he loved her. He knew now that he wanted to marry Heather Dean, marry her at once, if possible.

He put his arm around her shoulders and pulled her close to him, almost suffocating her. His lips pressed hard on hers; for a moment neither of them spoke because they lost everything in this newly found happiness.

When Ronnie eventually released her, he said.

'Darling, I have something to say and an important question to ask you.'

He kissed her passionately again and then broke out with, 'I love you as I have never loved or will never love another woman. Tell me, Heather darling, do you love me?'

Before she could answer he said:

'Damn...!'

His exclamation had been occasioned by a

knock which heralded the coming in of Marie.

The Frenchwoman didn't sense anything out of the ordinary as she entered, saying, 'Ready, Heather?'

Suddenly she noticed her employer.

'Oh, I'm sorry? Have I interrupted your conversation with Heather? Was it important?'

'My talks with Heather are always important.'

He smiled into the young girl's eyes and added:

'Good night, Heather dear. You must be tired and Marie is waiting. I'll see you in the morning.'

Marie answered, 'Yes, worse luck! Daddy Harcourt has got us on parade for a rehearsal!'

Ronnie smiled at Marie and pressed Heather's hand as he held open the door for the two girls to pass out.

Heather followed Marie to the car feeling that she was in a blissful dream. Hadn't the man she adored told her that he loved her?

As she was getting off to sleep that night Heather Dean speculated about the question that Ronnie was going to ask her had they not been interrupted by Marie. She felt sure that Ronnie had been on the point of asking her to marry him.

That night Heather went off to sleep feeling very happy, because she recalled Ronnie's words: 'I love you as I have never loved or will love another woman.'

She looked forward to the morrow with pleasurable anticipation.

CHAPTER TWENTY

Dr. Martin West's morning surgery opened at nine and Heather Dean was one of the first of the doctor's patients.

After a few opening remarks the doctor found himself in the situation of having to give the answer to a difficult question – a question that he had long dreaded.

He had asked Heather how she was feeling and she had admitted that occasionally she felt a slight pain in the arm that had been injured. 'If I sit in a draught my right arm aches,' she said.

Then he had asked her to do some simple arm-exercises, concluding with the direction: 'Stretch upwards as high as possible.'

He criticised. 'A bit stiff still, but you are getting on well. Continue with your exercises. Go on attending hospital for heat and movement treatment.'

All at once across Heather's mind flashed a picture of the 'limbering-up' exercises in the *corps de ballet*.

Something made her ask, 'Will I ever be

able to dance in ballet again?'

Dr. West did not answer for a minute or two. He sat studying his patient. He noticed that, today, there was a happy expression in her eyes and a glow about the girl that experience had taught him usually meant one thing – *she loved and was loved.*

For a minute he evaded answering her question.

At length he explained. 'The accident that you have incurred will not prevent you taking a sedentary job or leading an ordinary life. Nor will it unfit you in any way from being a wife or a mother.'

'But I can never be a ballet dancer again?'

The doctor avoided giving a direct answer.

'You are very young, and so it's very hard for a doctor to look far ahead and prophesy; also I should think that a beautiful and attractive girl like yourself will find everything to satisfy her in a happy marriage.'

Heather felt that she wanted to confide in the kind man who was facing her.

She said, 'Last night the man I love told me that he had never loved, nor would he ever love any other woman, *as he loved me.*'

The doctor smiled. 'I'm so glad that things are turning out in a satisfactory way for you and that you are happily settling your problems. Marry the man you love, my dear, and may you be very happy.'

Heather turned frank eyes on the surgeon.

She answered, 'Last night after Ronnie had told me that he loved me we were interrupted – shortly afterwards I had to say good night to him because a woman-friend was waiting to run me home in her car.'

'But you will be seeing your man-friend soon again?'

'Oh, yes, later on this morning.'

Dr. West smiled. 'Well, I hope everything will come right for you! Please accept my congratulations.'

Heather said in rather a wistful way, 'Ronnie hasn't actually asked me to marry him yet. As I have told you, we were interrupted last night by Marie coming into the room.'

'Don't worry, my dear; I feel that you'll be engaged by the time you next pay me a visit. Now, tell me, does the thought that you may never dance again grieve you intensely?'

'Not now. Some weeks ago if I had been told that I would never dance again, well, I think it would have killed me. However, when Ronnie told me last night that he loved me, well, everything changed, somehow life held new values for me.'

'Sensible girl! Well, now I hope that you'll

soon marry the man you love and be very happy. But now to the immediate present. I want you to keep up exercising your right hand and arm. Remember you can't exercise it too much. Avoid draughts and damp and see that you keep your right hand and arm warm.'

The surgeon rose and Heather felt that the interview was at an end.

Dr. West held out his hand, saying:

'Again, I want to congratulate you. May you and the man of your choice be very happy.'

Heather walked away from the doctor's surgery feeling that she was treading on air.

On reaching her flat she put on a kettle to make herself a cup of tea.

While she was waiting for the tea to draw she got a coat out of the wardrobe because she knew it would be the early hours before she returned home again.

As she let herself out the front door she was sorry to see that the day had changed. The sun had gone in and a cold wind had sprung up. Then came an unexpected shower. Heather's hair got wet through before she could get to shelter. She had put on her coat but her head, legs and feet had got soaked.

The feeling of dampness and discomfort affected Heather's spirits. All at once the images of Carmen and of Foster Jepson came into her mind. These disturbing thoughts made her momentarily forget that Ronnie had told her of his love. She started conjuring up a picture of Ronnie married to Carmen or some other woman. This was pure torture to the young girl.

Then she remembered that there were obstacles to her marriage with Ronald Steele.

And so with the disturbing images of Carmen and Foster Jepson in her mind, Heather entered the front door of the Delkushla club.

CHAPTER TWENTY-ONE

Mr. Harcourt had called a rehearsal for late morning. It was then found that Carmen was missing.

A search of the Spaniard's dressing-room revealed that she had taken away all her belongings. Her departure caused a great deal of comment, but not much surprise. Carmen was so unbalanced and erratic that somehow no one expected her to behave normally.

William Harcourt held a public enquiry to find out if anyone in the club knew what had happened to Carmen. He said jocosely:

'Are any of the men missing?'

There was a guffaw at this, and he followed it with the question, 'Did anyone see Carmen leave the club last night?'

Ronnie looked over at his friend. Ali's face was inscrutable. Whatever the Indian had to say would be for Mr. Harcourt's ears alone.

Somehow the excitement around Heather left her quite cold. The fact that Carmen had gone seemed too good to be true. But there was still the question of Foster Jepson. He seemed to be always coming back into her life and worrying her. Jepson's insinuations that he, Foster Jepson, had, in a sinister way shared her past – all this could not have escaped a clever man like her employer. Heather was afraid.

She tried to comfort herself with the thought that on the preceding night Ronnie had said that he loved her. However, she worried in case Ronnie Steele's affection for her would change when he learnt about her strange adventures in Nice. If Ronnie changed towards her and got engaged to another girl Heather knew that she would not be able to stay for another minute at the Delkushla. However, she now realised that life, indeed, would be empty, were Ronald Steele to go out of it.

Ronnie noticed Heather's listless manner and the unhappy expression in her eyes. What a contrast, he thought, to the joyous look on her face on the previous night when he told her of his love.

A great wave of affection and pity for Heather swept over the young club owner. He realised that he must make Heather tell him what role Foster Jepson had played in her past. Ronnie felt that the financier was an evil man – one that must be debarred from entering the Delkushla. However, he felt that he could do nothing till Heather told him exactly what had happened in Nice between her and Foster Jepson.

When the morning's rehearsal was over Ronnie waited for Heather Dean as she came off the stage.

'Come out to lunch with me,' he invited, 'I have something important to say to you, and I feel that we can talk best if we are out of the building. I mean, we may be overheard here if we talk confidentially.'

Heather's face had lit up at Ronnie's invitation. 'I'll love to come out to lunch with you,' she answered.

It was only a few minutes' walk to a quiet little restaurant off the beaten track. The tables were set in alcoves which gave the diners privacy.

'I like this place because it's so fresh and bright looking.' Heather smiled as she said this.

'Yes, and there's no chance of anyone overhearing what we say. Now, dear, here's the menu, so please choose what you fancy.'

It was an excellent lunch, and as the meal progressed Heather seemed more relaxed and the smile came back into her eyes.

When they had finished their coffee Ronnie made a suggestion.

'As the weather has changed for the better today – it's good to see the sun again, and as you are not due back to the Delkushla for several hours, let's make for a little park I know within walking distance of this restaurant. We can sit and chat there. Also, there is a restaurant in the grounds so we can have tea later on.'

In rather an apathetic way Heather agreed.

They got two seats in a secluded place.

For some time they sat and smoked in almost a complete silence.

As soon as Heather had finished her cigarette, Ronnie threw his on the ground and stubbed it out with the toe of his shoe.

Suddenly he bent and kissed Heather on her lips.

It began as a glancing kiss, a light casually happy kiss. Ronnie now caught Heather breathlessly close, so it became a kiss which cleaved, shattered and left them quite speechless, still swept around by the love which had quickened.

He said softly, 'Heather, I love you dearly, and I feel that you are secretly troubled and that your worries and unhappiness are connected with Foster Jepson and also with your stay in Nice. Please tell me everything.'

As she hesitated he went on: 'I want to fight your battles and take care of you, and I can't do this if you don't tell me everything. Foster Jepson said that he had known you in Nice. Now, dearest, tell me how you met him?'

CHAPTER TWENTY-TWO

'I first saw Foster Jepson at Nice,' Heather started. 'Our ballet company had been three weeks at Monte Carlo; now we had a fortnight's booking at Nice. As this was my first experience of the sun-drenched Riviera, with its wealth of flowers and beautiful blue Mediterranean sea, well, I just thought that I was in Heaven. At Monte Carlo I had been promoted. Owing to the sudden illness of one of the "Little Swans" I stepped into this dancer's place. At rehearsal time I had also been honoured because I was chosen as the understudy of the leading ballerina. So my future seemed rosy.'

She paused. Ronnie suggested:

'So you looked forward to a long and successful career as a ballerina?'

'Something like that! However, Fate was going to deal me a nasty blow.'

'From the hand of Foster Jepson? But please go on and tell me the circumstances in which you first came across this man.'

'Well, as I said a minute ago, I originally

met Foster Jepson in Nice. I had palled up with a girl called Valerie Trent. Our chaperon in the *corps de ballet* required that we did not live in an hotel or *pension*, alone; in the same way we were expected to go about the town in twos. Valerie and I put up at the hotel "Les Camelias" because it was clean and inexpensive. To make a further saving, we only had bed and breakfast at "Les Camelias". At our hotel, meals were served in the front garden and this restaurant was open to non-residents.

'In an interval during our third performance in Nice, Valerie drew my attention to a tall, slim, sinister-looking man sitting in the middle of the front row of the stalls.

'"That fellow has had that same seat for the last three performances and he never takes his eyes off me".' She was mistaken in her last remark, as she was to soon find out!

'To save money Valerie and I lunched and dined at a small café "Le chat noir". We patronised this place because it was near our hotel and a short walking distance from the theatre. Although the café was cheap the food was good. There was a curious atmosphere about the place. Madame and a waitress were the sole members of the staff of the café. Valerie said that both these women were bad characters and that there was something sinister about 'Le chat noir'. Later on I was to agree with Valerie.

'On the fourth day Valerie and I had only just sat down at a table when my companion whispered:

'"My admirer who sits in the middle of the front row in the theatre every night has just entered by the door, and he's making a bee-line for our table."

'She had scarcely finished saying this, when I looked up to encounter the gaze of the sinister-looking, tall, thin man. He addressed me.

'"My name is Foster Jepson. May I ask, are you Miss Mannering?"

'"No,"' I snapped the answer at him.

'"Well you are exactly like someone I knew called Lorna Mannering."

'I didn't answer, so he turned to Valerie and pulling out a gold cigarette case together with a gold lighter he offered, "Will you have a cigarette? It's good to meet compatriots when one is abroad, especially such talented Englishwomen like you ladies."

'I noticed that Valerie's eyes had been resting on the huge diamonds in the rings on Foster Jepson's fingers. My girl friend had repeatedly said to me that she was out for "a rich sugar-daddy" who would give her expensive presents and help her to become a *première* ballerina. So now she smiled at Foster Jepson and when he asked, "May I sit down?" she answered, "Why not?"

'Foster Jepson took the chair that Valerie indicated. He beckoned the waitress and insisted on treating Valerie and I to dinner. It was the best meal Valerie and I had ever eaten at "Le chat noir" but by the end of dinner Valerie was fuming. She felt affronted because Jepson had scarcely addressed a word to her. Over the table he tried to make love to me. I felt embarrassed because I found the man distasteful in every way.

'Next day Valerie accepted and encouraged the attentions of a French fan of hers, who was staying at "Les Camelias". I think she wanted to show me that *she,* too, could get an admirer. From that time onwards, Valerie deserted me at meal-times. Rather proudly she told me that her Frenchman now paid for her lunches and dinners.

'As "Le chat noir" was cheap and conveniently situated as to the theatre and my hotel, I continued to eat there. The drawback to this café was that from now on, Foster Jepson frequented it. However, I told him frankly that I liked eating alone, and that I had no intention of letting him pay for any of my meals. So I just gave him a curt nod when I saw him at the café.

'As the days passed by, I noticed a curious thing – Madame the proprietress was attempting to be very friendly. The first few days of my going to "Le chat noir" she just ignored my presence. Now she always smiled as I entered, and when I paid my bill at her desk she invariably made some friendly remark. She spoke good English. I attributed her friendly overtures to her Frenchwoman's business acumen – she welcomed me because now I was a regular customer.

'Our fortnight in Nice passed quickly. On my last full day when I entered the café to have a meal, before going on to the theatre, Madame brought me my meal. This surprised me because she rarely did any of the waiting. She smiled, and pointing to an empty chair said, "Do you mind if I sit down for a moment?"

'"Please take a seat, Madame. I shall miss your restaurant. Our *corps de ballet* moves to Paris tomorrow."

'"So I've heard, and because of your going I have a favour to ask you."

'I waited and the proprietress went on.

"You have been such a regular and such a pleasant customer, and so tomorrow I shall be honoured and delighted if you will be my guest for lunch? I shall cook you the specialities of my restaurant, and I'll toast your future success as a ballerina in the best wines of 'Le chat noir'. Everything will be, as you English say, 'on the house'. Please be my guest, mees."

'Madame seemed to be making such a point of the invitation that I felt it would be boorish to refuse.

'I smiled and said, "I accept your kind invitation with pleasure."

'"Well, will the usual time be convenient to you, mees?"

'"Yes, thanks. As our suitcases go in the baggage-van I shall have only myself to see to the station. Our train goes out at three."

'"Well, till tomorrow, mademoiselle. I'm afraid I must return to my desk now."

'When the proprietress had left me I looked around and saw to my relief that Foster Jepson was not in the restaurant.

'At the theatre that night I told Valerie about the invitation that Madame had given me.

'She shrugged her shoulders in a contemptuous way, saying:

'"You're welcome to your free meal at 'Le chat noir'. My André is giving me a slap-up lunch at a first-class restaurant."

'At the fall of the curtain that night our manager gave us our railway tickets, saying, "I take it that you have all followed instructions and brought your suitcases to the theatre so that your luggage can travel with the scenery, props, etc."

'As there was a murmur of assent he said, "Good! Well, now all you have to do is to catch the train tomorrow. If anyone is so foolish as to miss it he or she must follow by a later train".'

Here Heather paused, and laying her hand on Ronnie's remarked, 'I'm afraid this is rather a long tale. Am I boring you, Ronnie?'

'Oh, no! I'm deeply interested. *Please* go on.'

'Well, next day when I entered the café at noon Madame met me with outstretched hands.

'"As you are my guest," she said, "you must eat in my private room today – please excuse me."

'She led the way through the door at the far end of the restaurant into a small sitting-room where the table was laid for a meal. There was a serving hatch to the kitchen on the left-hand side. Through this Madame fetched and served a most appetising meal for me and herself. There was a carafe of wine on the table and from it she poured out a glass of sparkling wine, I found the drink very heady but I finished it and not to offend madame I let her refill my glass.

'At the end of the meal the proprietress carried our used dishes over to the service hatch.

'She spoke in a low tone of voice, in French, to the person who was the other side of the hatch, but I could not understand what she was saying.

'Coming back to me she smiled, and patting a place on the divan, said:

'"Come and sit here, chérie. My presence is urgently required in the kitchen, but I won't be more than a minute, and while I am there I shall make our coffee and you will say that it is the best coffee you have ever tasted. Come! sit here and be comfortable. Do have a smoke while you're waiting.'

'I obeyed her and she placed a cushion behind my head and lighted a cigarette for me.

'"Un instant!' Madame darted over to the sideboard that was behind me. I couldn't see what she was doing, but I heard the sound of liquid being poured into glasses.

'In a minute she was back, facing me again, a glass filled with wine in each hand.

'"You must drink a toast with me. It is to your happiness. This wine is the best and most expensive in the café."

'She held up her glass and said:

'"May you have great success in your career and one day be the greatest of ballerinas. Salut!" She threw her head back, tossed off the glass and said, "To bring about the lucky spell you, too, must empty your glass."

'She laughed and so did I. With an effort I did so.

'Instantly the room seemed to be swimming about me. The last thing I heard before I drifted off into unconsciousness was Madame saying:

'"Lie back against the cushions, chérie. I shall go and get your coffee".'

Heather stopped speaking.

Ronnie questioned, 'And then?'

'Well, I knew no more till I felt someone touching me. I opened my eyes and saw that it was Madame Chevreux, the proprietress of the hotel "Les Camelias".

'Madame Chevreux put a small tray which held coffee, rolls and butter on my bedside table. She then went over to the window and pulled aside the curtain. The morning light fell on my small travelling clock and I saw that it was nine o'clock.

'Madame handed me a cup of coffee.

'"How are you feeling this morning?"

'"Feeling? Oh, my head is aching."

'"I'm not surprised."

'The tone of the Frenchwoman's voice had a brusque and displeased note in it.

'My head ached as I tried to remember. I asked, "But what am I doing back here in your hotel? Yesterday morning I paid my bill and said good-bye to you..."

'She remained silent.

'So I burst out with, "But what happened? I should have gone on the three o'clock train to Paris!"

'Madame Chevreux shrugged her shoulders. She said in curt tones:

'"Well, shortly after midnight when the night porter was collecting any glasses left on the tables in the garden restaurant he found you slumped in one of the armchairs in a dark part of the garden. Luckily I had not gone to bed, so when the man called me I came along and I found that you were insensible and smelt strongly of drink. The porter carried you up to your bedroom and

I undressed you."

'The strong coffee was clearing my head. I protested:

'"But, madame, I only had two glasses of wine at lunch. It was at the 'Le chat noir'."

'Madame said in thoughtful tones, "That restaurant has a very bad name. But now, Miss Dean, eat up your breakfast. Your job is to join your company in Paris as soon as possible."

'"Oh! yes I'll get up and dress at once."

'Suddenly I remembered what, in my hurry, I had forgotten to do yesterday. I turned to Madame Chevreux and asked, "Would you be so kind as to give my room-maid the tip I forgot to leave yesterday?"

'Certainly. Do you want your bag?'

'I nodded, and she went over to the dressing-table for it.

'When I opened my bag I gave a cry.

'"Is anything wrong?"

'"Yes, Madame Chevreux. Look! My purse has gone, and so has my wallet."

'"What was in your wallet?"

'"My passport and my ticket to Paris."

'A flush came on Madame's face.

'"Are you insinuating that my porter has stolen your things?"

'"No, I think I was drugged and robbed at

'Le chat noir' café!"

'I jumped out of bed and started to dress quickly.

'"Where are you going, Miss Dean?"

'"To the café. There may be an innocent explanation. When I fell unconscious those things may have fallen out of my bag."

'Madame shook her head. "Someone brought you back in an unconscious state to 'Les Camelias' and left you in our garden. Take care of yourself at 'Le chat noir' – it has a bad name."

'In spite of Madame's warning, within an hour I had entered "Le chat noir". The place was practically empty. I addressed the sullen-looking waitress. I demanded to see the proprietress. The girl said:

'"You cannot see her, she is busy."

'"All right! I'll go to the police."

'"*Un instant!*" She went through the door and returned with the proprietress.'

Heather paused.

'What was the result of all this?' Ronnie asked.

'Madame took me into her private room. When I questioned her about yesterday's events and mentioned that my purse and wallet were missing from my bag she flew into a towering rage and denied having ever seen me before. She called in the servant and the young French girl also said that I had never called at "Le chat noir". While I was speaking to the waitress madame went away and I could hear that she was phoning someone. I think it must have been Foster Jepson, because when I got out into the street he was there waiting for me.

'When I repeated my charges about being drugged and robbed at "Le chat noir", he said:

'"Leave everything to me. I'll make things right for you."

'When I demanded what was I to do, he answered, "My beautiful, you are in a bad spot, in fact I can't think of a worse situation for an English girl than to be stranded in a continental country, without a passport and without money."

'"What am I to do?"

'"Just place yourself in my hands. I'm deeply attracted by your beauty. You are the most attractive girl I've ever met. I've a house near Nice – it will be your home. I'll give you as much money as you want and lovely clothes and jewels. A beautiful woman should have a beautiful setting and I'll see that you get this."

'"At a price!"

'"Well, my Lovely One, I can't marry you because I already have a wife."

'He pointed across the road. "My car is parked the other side of the street so let's go."

'He put his hand on my arm. I shook it off.

'Foster Jepson said, "Don't be a lovely little silly. Don't you see you're cornered? There is nothing you can do."

'"Oh yes there is! And if you try to stop me I'll scream hard, and when the police come I'll make accusations against you and against the proprietress of 'Le chat noir'."'

Heather stopped speaking.

Ronnie helped her, by asking, 'What was the result of all this?'

'I went straight to the theatre where the manager and some of the staff recognised me. I told the manager everything and he phoned the English consul. The latter sent an official to the theatre to first question me and later to take me to the Consul. A long-distance call was put through to the manager of the *corps de ballet* in Paris. The Consul told the manager that as he believed my story was true he was providing me with money and a ticket to Paris together with a temporary passport. Finally the manager promised to send a member of the company to meet my train at the Paris terminus. An official belonging to the English consulate put me on the train that my manager had specified and Valerie and one of the male members of the company met me at the Paris railway terminus.'

'Was everything all right after that?' demanded Ronnie.

'Far from it! I had missed a matinée and so a substitute had to be found for my role as one of the "Little Swans".

'I heard later that Valerie had told everyone that I stayed behind in Nice because I was having an *affaire* with a man. Even when I got to Paris and told her of my losses she went on with her malicious gossip because she told the manager that I must have been dead drunk and just lost my valuables.'

'But surely your employer didn't believe Valerie?'

'Nothing I could say or do could convince him that I was a reliable member of his company. As you know, I was not re-engaged.'

As Heather seemed on the point of tears Ronnie put his hand caressingly on hers. 'Don't worry, my sweet. All that is past. Let's forget it.'

Ronnie was silent for a moment and then

he said:

'There's just one thing I don't understand. It's this: How did Foster Jepson trace you to the Delkushla?'

'Well, there again it was due to the evil genius of Valerie. Foster Jepson told me he wrote to Valerie Trent care of the ballet company. He put in a stamped envelope asking her for my address. He added that as Valerie gave him Madame Eglantine's name and address he called on Madame Eglantine. Madame, thinking that she was doing me a good turn, told Jepson of my accident and how I now had a job at the Delkushla night club. Well, as you know, the result was that Foster Jepson called at your club and started worrying me.'

Ronnie nodded. 'I wouldn't be at all surprised if Jepson approached Carmen and offered her money if she could make mischief between you and me so as to separate us for ever.'

Heather then told Ronnie what she knew on that point.

While Heather had been speaking Ronnie had been studying her intently. She looked so young and so unsophisticated. She was curiously ignorant of the sordid things of life. He contrasted her with girls of her own age whom he had met and he knew that compared to them she was ignorant as to sex experience. In that affair at Nice Ronnie realised that Heather had been the victim of a nasty plot, luckily for her one that failed.

Ronald remembered the evil, sex-ridden face of Foster Jepson. He guessed that Jepson's *affaires* had been numerous and the young club owner determined that the financier would never have the chance to see Heather again.

When Heather had finished her tale Ronnie bent over and kissed her again.

He said, 'Don't you worry any more about Foster Jepson. As soon as we get back to the club I'll get in touch with my lawyer and he will see that Jepson never comes to the Delkushla again or in any way worries you.'

'Thank you, Ronnie.' She wondered if he was doing this just because he liked doing kind acts, or because he really loved her? She was soon to know.

He seemed to read her thoughts. A sudden idea struck him. He asked:

'Darling, have you ever heard of Georgian Bay?'

Heather shook her head.

'Well, it's a lovely part of Canada in Northern Ontario and north of Toronto. It's all lakes and islands, full of deer and birds and the fishing is superb. It's called the sportsman's paradise but it's the lover's paradise too. Well, my sweet, we're going to Georgian Bay for our honeymoon. Oh my darling, how I love you and how happy we'll be!'

There was no sound from the girl in his arms and suddenly the young man realised that she had not accepted him. A great fear took possession of Ronald. But it was banished when Heather smiled and asked:

'When does the next boat leave for Canada?'

The publishers hope that this book has given you enjoyable reading. Large Print Books are especially designed to be as easy to see and hold as possible. If you wish a complete list of our books please ask at your local library or write directly to:

Dales Large Print Books
Magna House, Long Preston,
Skipton, North Yorkshire.
BD23 4ND

This Large Print Book, for people
who cannot read normal print,
is published under the auspices of

THE ULVERSCROFT FOUNDATION

... we hope you have enjoyed this book.
Please think for a moment about those
who have worse eyesight than you ...
and are unable to even read or enjoy
Large Print without great difficulty.

You can help them by sending a
donation, large or small, to:

**The Ulverscroft Foundation,
1, The Green, Bradgate Road,
Anstey, Leicestershire, LE7 7FU,
England.**
or request a copy of our brochure for
more details.

The Foundation will use all donations
to assist those people who are visually
impaired and need special attention
with medical research, diagnosis
and treatment.

Thank you very much for your help.